DISTURBED BY HER SONG

DISTURBED BY HER SONG

Tanith Lee

writing **as** *and* **with**

Esther Garber

&

Judas Garbah

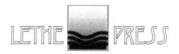

LETHE PRESS

Published in 2010 by LETHE PRESS
118 Heritage Avenue • Maple Shade, NJ 08052-3018
www.lethepressbooks.com • lethepress@aol.com
ISBN: 1-59021-311-4
ISBN-13: 978-1-59021-311-7

This is a work of fiction. Names, characters, places, and incidents are products of the author's imagination or are used fictitiously.

Set in Adobe Garamond, Desdemona, & Harrington.
Cover art: David Gilmore.
Cover design: Thomas Drymon, drymondesign.
Interior design: Alex Jeffers.

LIBRARY OF CONGRESS
CATALOGING-IN-PUBLICATION DATA

Lee, Tanith.
 Disturbed by her song / Tanith Lee, writing as and with Esther Garber & Judas Garbah.
    p. cm.
 A collection of dark and fantastical stories.
 ISBN-13: 978-1-59021-311-7 (pbk. : alk. paper)
 ISBN-10: 1-59021-311-4 (pbk. : alk. paper)
 I. Title.
 PR6062.E4163D57 2010
 823'.914--dc22

                                        2010025907

MEETING THE GARBERS

I first met the Garbers in the 1990s; that is, I met Esther, and her brother, Judas. Anna didn't turn up, though she subsequently sent me a polite and kindly note. In fact I've *never* met Anna, not yet, despite being given access to certain portions of her own work, and recently one of Judas's stories which, it seems, she assembled from Judean fragments.

Esther's first communication with me involved the viewing of a headstone.

This was an arresting event. She refers to it in her novel, *34*, but allowed me to see the stone first. Just as the novel describes it, it was carved, and of very new-looking marble, set above a neatly finished grave. It bore only the number that became the book's title.

The complete novel was given to me shortly after. And not a great time after that, the first collection – *Fatal Women* – followed. Some separate stories by Judas arrived a few years after *Fatal*, and were not included in the initial Esther collection. (Judas doesn't seem to care about this. He always refers to himself as 'a Writer' – but does he mean by trade – or inclination? Has he been published elsewhere? I sense some subterranean work, via a small press of long ago, in French, or even an Arabic language.)

Back in the '90s, the Garbers were rather striking. (They still are, I would say.) Judas especially was, and remains, a very handsome man, naturally slim and quite tall, by now, I would guess, in his sixties, as I am. But time frames with – definitely Esther

– are hard to fix. Her (and Anna's) childhoods at least appear to have taken place in Egypt in the 1920s-1930s; but then Esther also proposes a young womanhood in England and France, between the two World Wars. By the mid-90s she should therefore (yes?) have been approaching or inhabiting, at least, her seventieth year – or her *hundredth*! But she looked to me then of a youthful appearance – approximately fifty. She still, I have to remark, does. A smart and well-dressed woman, neither old-fashioned nor let-me-be-of-the-Now, she shows her ethnicity – presumably mostly Jewish; this less in her (excellent) pale complexion, grey eyes and lush, wavy dark brown hair (not a hint of grey in *that*) than in a sort of antique-coin type arrangement of her profile. Semitic she is. Judas, too, of course. He is besides a seemingly wonderful equality of half Jew and half Arab, with the definite resultant beauty. His hair is mostly still black, his eyes, if anything, blacker than before.

Neither of these people is especially warm and forthcoming however. They are cool, if sometimes observant and witty companions. Both are quite guarded also. Curious, it always seems to me, when their writing is so determinedly open and *frank*.

They have, they did from the inception, make very clear the different spelling of their surname. Esther, of course, is *Garber*, which is recognizably European Jewish. Judas meanwhile spells his version *Garbah*. I haven't been able to learn if this is based on some variant, presumably adopted by his butterfly mother, or an invention of his own.

I firmly believe that both of them are not merely compulsively truthful, in the way less of the Confessional than of certain writers/story-tellers, but conversely strategic liars. I'm well aware too that neither of them will object to my saying this. (Would I dare say it otherwise?) Lying also has its part in an authorial work-kit.

They do, perhaps inevitably, fascinate me. And whatever they care to reveal, demonstrate, *tell* me, I find enormously interesting.

There is Esther's London (UK) flat, for instance. (It has a brief manifestation in an earlier story not appearing in these volumes.) A weird apartment in its way, with a huge main room divided by a single step into an upper and lower 'terrace,' and with much smaller rooms – kitchen, bathroom, workroom, bedroom – leading off a gallery above. It has long windows and green curtains, and a view outside of tall, summer-rich trees and grayish stone, one of those inner London streets you suddenly find around Harley Street, the British Museum, or otherwhere. Between the apartment door and the outer front door to the flat, is a 'storage' area (what exactly is stored there?) that also has a small guest bedroom with bed and en-suite lavatory and shower. Esther parks her brother out there on his very occasional visits. She has said he has repeatedly requested she acquire a cat, so that he can admire and stroke it, when in residence. But she hasn't done so, and Judas denies all this. There is always a little scratchiness from both of them, when referring to the other. Or to Anna, actually. It can be seen anyway quite plainly in the text.

As for Anna – as I say, I've never glimpsed her. She seems a well-organized, clever, possibly erudite woman, any hang-ups, (as evinced through Esther's *34*, etc) either well under control or – maybe – non-existent. She respects her sister's and her half-brother's (Judas is only related to these women through their father) literary work, but has her own agenda. She is far more successfully secretive than either of them. And too Esther's implication (in her novel) that Anna is – how shall I say? – *less* than she seems – may be indicative. I wonder if I ever *will* be allowed, or even able, to meet her? I'm unsure, if given the chance, whether I'll be eager – or dismayed.

Having said which, obviously, I have never met any of these three in the flesh. In the flesh, so far as I can tell, they do not exist. At least not in any form or body I have ever physically encountered.

Nevertheless, to state they are simply three more of the thousands of characters I myself have written about, or through whose *minds* I have been made privy to their lives, seems not to express any sort of truth at all. Though I would proclaim this in reference to any character of whom I've written – they are all real to me, more real, *far* more real than so-called Reality – yet with the

Garbers some other categorization must be found. I haven't yet found one. And for this reason, their narratives, which I undeniably write (long-hand, as ever), then type, are styled – for the sake of veracity, *never* obscuration or gimmick: *Tanith Lee writing as Esther Garber/Judas Garbah*.

That they are both gay is decidedly not the reason. I have written about Lesbian and male homosexual aspiration, love, lust and longing in several other places. Just as I've written about and as, 'straight' women and men, gifted sorcerers, murderers, gods, demons and saints – and anything else I felt, at the time, given to encompass.

Nor do I think I *do* write about E and J because they and I share Jewish blood. (I'm a mix – half Russian Jew, a quarter English – with a tiny dash of French – a quarter County Clare Irish, and with a feasible whisker of Russian, and a drop of Black blood – unluckily the last two are probably untraceable.) But Esther and Judas, (and I assume Anna) are far more proper exponents of the Semitic races than I am. E and J at least have the correct looks – as I said before, that glamour you can still see on ancient coins. And they are far more seasoned, steeped in other countries and customs, for example, those of France, Spain and Egypt.

They are not me. *They* – are *themselves*.

Evidently, in this perceivably split-personality tract, I am both distancing myself and irrevocably attaching myself to the Garbers. But then, as with most of my characters, and in this instance far more than with any other, they too have attached themselves to *me*. When they are there (often they are absent), they are clearly delineated presences, just *outside* the mindscape. And unlike the others, too, they remain largely clandestine.

How much more work they will give me I have no idea. I've never sensed a forthcoming library, not even a full shelf. I know there should be one more Esther novel. I even know the title: *Cleopatra at the Blue Hotel*. This promises to reveal how Esther and Judas first met, as adults, by the Nile. While a second collection of Esther stories and novellas, which includes some pieces by Judas, plus the odd half-glimpse of Anna, already exists. Two of these tales, incidentally, Esther and I wrote together. Lee is truly bats, one might say. Or not. It seemed to me those particular tales have a combined perspective. Certain things I could essay through Esther that wouldn't otherwise have occurred to me, and (maybe?) vice versa.

To go back to the first introduction and meeting: despite not taking place corporeally, it did begin through a viewing of that pure white headstone. I dreamed of it, in the 1990s, complete with its number: 34. In many Dream Books, a clean, well-kept grave can be interpreted as a brand new start. I took it as such. And about three weeks after began to write the novel with that name. I had the first sentence, and I had the sense of Esther Garber. Nothing more was needed.

More even than with all the differing kinds of fiction I write, the Garbers have given me a significantly *unlike* territory. *In* this world, and out of it, anachronistic (deliberately), time-twisting, utterly self-indulgent – why not? Why write in chains? – and experimental. Varnished truth and gloves-off lies: the exquisite question that never has an answer; the answer that *is* the question.

Thank you, Madame et Monsieur.

—Tanith Lee, 2009

CONTENTS

Once upon a time there was a princess, outside whose high bedroom window a nightingale sang every night from a pomegranate tree.

While the nightingale sang, the princess slept deeply and well, dreaming of wondrous and beautiful things. However there came a night when the nightingale, for reasons of her own, did not sing but flew far away.

In the morning the princess summoned a gardener and told him to cut down the pomegranate tree. The man protested; the tree was a fine one, young, healthy and fruitful. But the princess would not relent. For as she said, all that one previous night a nightingale had perched in the branches, and the princess's sleep had been very much disturbed by her song.

Eastern Tales
translated by Anna Garber

Youth and Age

BLACK EYED SUSAN

Esther Garber

Black Eyed Susan first passed me in the corridor, just after the old woman had pushed me into it. Black Eyed Susan's eyes were black as ink from outer space, and she stared a moment, coldly with them, at me. But the old woman was still there, poking the twigs of her fingers into my side.

"What? What is it?" I mumbled to her. I had become confused, but already Black Eyed Susan had turned the corridor corner and was lost to view.

"In there," rasped the old woman.

"Where? Why?"

"There, *there.*"

Across the corridor was a door, one of many. "There?"

Like a mouse all in black, though not a black like Black Eyed Susan's, the old woman continued to push me forward as if I were on wheels, towards the door.

It was marked *Private.*

"But—" I said.

Sharply, leaning past me, she rapped on the door with her horn-rimmed knuckles. For a mouse, the old woman was quite large, but for a woman quite small, shriveled down nearly to a husk, but a hard one.

From within the room a male voice said, "Enter. If you must."

The old woman turned the handle of the door, thrust me through, and slammed it at my back.

A big, warm room, fire in its grate, armchairs strewn about. Behind a polished desk piled with ledgers and papers, a man of average age and some indications of wealth, eyed me over his spectacles.

"Who are you?" he inquired, without interest.

"My name is Esther Garber."

"And?"

"I've come to work at the hotel."

"And so?"

"Monsieur, I was pushed into this room by an old woman."

"Ah!" A bark of laughter burst, beneath his narrow mustache. "Granny at her old tricks."

"Oh, was it your grandmother then, Monsieur?"

He drew himself up, removed his glasses, and scanned me intently. "I am the Patron. This hotel is mine. Normally you'd have no dealings with me. All that is seen to by Madame Ghoule, whom, I assume, you have already met when hired. However, the old lady you refer to, Madame Cora, will tend to drag to my notice any new girl on the staff I might, she supposes, fancy."

My face became blank. I met his eyes with all the hauteur of Black Eyed Susan's. Knowing, nevertheless, that if he must have me, then he must, since it was generally the safest way. Besides. I needed the job here, lowly as it was. My money had run out; and beyond the clean windows of the Patron's boudoir, light snow was already falling on the little French town.

He said, smiling with disdain, "Well, what do you think?"

"I'm surprised," I said, manifesting I hoped a halfway ordinary feminine reaction.

"Don't be," said the Patron. "My grandmother is mad, of course. Anyway, you're not my type—" what he actually said was, *not my bite of biscuit.*

I should now be modestly insulted, perhaps. I lowered my gaze, and thought of ink-black eyes, floating there between me and the patterned carpet.

He said. "What did you say your name was?"

"Esther."

"And your duties here?"

"Bar work, and some kitchen work, so I was told."

"And why then are you up here at the top of my hotel – aside, of course, from Madame Cora, who will have waylaid you somewhere between here and the ground floor?"

"I'm to sleep at the hotel, so Madame Ghoule informed me."

"Of course. Very well then. I wish you a pleasant stay," incongruously he added.

So I was dismissed, opened the door and came out, looking uneasily about for mad Madame Cora. But there was now no sign of her, no sign of anyone.

The entire hotel, which called itself *The Queen*, had a forlorn winter appearance, and few guests. Madame Ghoule, for it had been she who interviewed me, was a formidable barrel of a woman. The interview had consisted of her terse remarks on my proposed duties, and the evidence that I looked too skinny to be able to do any of it; was I therefore strong enough? I lied that I was, which she at once accepted. "You will keep no tips for yourself for the first fortnight, that is our policy here. I hope that is understood." I said it was. "After that you will receive your portion of tips from the communal dish." I knew, having done such work previously, the 'portion' would amount to only slightly more than the initial fortnight's nil.

Walking back along the corridor, I found myself, instead of taking the back stair downwards to my allotted room, turning the corner. But Black Eyed Susan had vanished entirely. She might be in any of the rooms, or none. I knocked quietly on each closed door I now passed. But stopped this after one was suddenly flung open, and an irate man in shirtsleeves cried, "Have you brought my beer? Where is my beer?" I apologized, and told him it would shortly arrive. "I have been waiting here half my life," he ranted, "for one tankard of bloody beer!"

Below, on the third floor, when I reached it, I located my room. The bed had been made up – then unmade and left open – and the sheets seemed to have been slept in only that morning. Some longish, dark brown hairs lay on the pillow, and bending over it, I inhaled a faint musk of violets.

Hadn't just such a scent wafted by me in the wake of Black Eyed Susan?

I thought, with abrupt alarmed excitement, that maybe she and I were to share this room. The bed was easily wide enough. But there were no personal items put about (aside from the dark hairs). It was an awful room, in fact. Bare floorboards, on which somebody had thrown a single rough shabby towel to act as a rug, an overhead electric light without a shade. The windows had tawdry curtains, and outside the town was settling grimly into the icing of the snow.

I made the bed again, and went along to the bathroom, which lay another floor down. Only the cold tap would run, though the hot made urgent chugging noises. I did the best I could with myself, then went back all the way downstairs.

The bar, where I was to begin, was in the charge of a tall, thin woman. She sat in a sort of open kiosk to one side sewing things, which changed color over the days and nights, from white to red to grey, but which even so never revealed their intentions. To me they looked most like bags for octopuses. Nevertheless, despite the octopus bags, she kept her scalpel of an eye on the room, calling out with no warning, in a shrill voice, either to me or the male waiter: "Window table wants serving. Make haste with the coffee." Such things. The customers, who came and went from the street outside, or ambled in from the hotel itself, tipped her in preference to us, and I saw the loot always go directly into her pocket. Her name was Mademoiselle Coudeban.

At intervals I was retrieved from the bar to wash up dishes or floors, scrape potatoes and peel onions, or pour boiling water on beetles below the sinks. After a day or two, I was also sent to lay tables, and next carry plates into the restaurant, under the large, chilly eyes of the Chief Waiter.

At six, midday and seven in the evening, I ate in the kitchen, at one edge of a littered table. These meals were gratis, but consisted of soup, bread, and sometimes cheese. Three chambermaids also came down to feed in this way, but they were given pieces of pies or meats already prepared for the paying customers. I was obviously too new for this treat.

The chambermaids questioned me eagerly. I was a fresh face, and apparently they longed to hear of other venues. But I didn't make the grave error of saying I had come from anywhere fascinating. I made myself as dull as possible. Nor would I take sides in their instantaneously conjured arguments. Soon they were offended with me and left me alone, only murmuring the odd sulky slight behind their hands.

Black Eyed Susan, however, did not appear in the kitchen, nor any other place. All that first day, evening and night, until I was cast out of the bar at two in the morning, part of me was alert as a pair of raised antennae. But there was no trace of her at all. Finally I asked Jean, the bar waiter, if anyone else worked in the hotel, aside from the people I had seen. He answered me that of course no one else was there, what did I expect, in winter?

When at last I crawled upstairs that first night-morning, washed in the cold water, and went to my icy little room, no one was there either.

I hadn't put anything out in the room myself, partly for fear the few things I had might be stolen. The space looked miserly empty, and quite frozen in the snow-light from beyond the window. All that day the snow had descended, and been tramped for proof into the hotel. Now the town lay like a white desert. A scatter of lights burned on in distant white humps that might be houses, or only hills. Far above a scornful moon loitered in the clearing sky. Dogs barked to each other and fell silent. Cars had been banished from the roads.

The hotel however snuffled in its half-sleep. And all around a muffled roaring blew about, which might be the hot water pipes of the heating system, which worked, doubtless, everywhere but in my room.

I knew I'd better go to bed. Tomorrow I must find more blankets and perhaps an old-fashioned stone hot water-bottle.

Under the cold sheet I lay rigid, tempted to snivel at my plight, which was all my own fault anyway. But sleep overtook me before tears could. I woke at a quarter to six to the alarm call of someone thumping on my door.

"Are we on fire?" I shouted. "Go away."

"Such impertinence!" shouted back Madame Ghoule.

It turned out it was her duty to arouse from slumber all the girls who worked at *The Queen*. Having herself retired to bed at ten-thirty, I'm sure she sadistically enjoyed her morning task.

Days and nights passed then in this way. It was true I learnt the names of the three maids – Sylvie, Claude and Jasmine. I was also propositioned by one or two male customers in the bar, evaded them, and was told off by Mademoiselle Octopus – whether because she thought I'd said yes, or because I refused, I wasn't quite certain.

The snow remained on the town, sealing us in a white envelope of inertia.

On my fifth evening, I saw the man from the upper corridor, the one whose door I had knocked on, and who had flown up honking for beer like a desperate goose.

He draped himself at the bar counter, and peered at Jean, who was presiding over the bottles of absinthe and cognac.

"Say, Jeanot, I want to ask you something."

"Yes, Monsieur?" Jean was always polite to guests.

"It's a bit tricky. You see, there is a woman I clapped eyes on, up in the top corridor. A real—" he lowered his voice to protect the room, though not myself, who was stood there not two feet from him – "eyeful. A stunner. Could be from Paris. Thick brown hair tied back very neat, and a brownish skin. Black eyes. Black as coal. And a figure – well. And her legs, Jeanot. What legs those are. It was the other day when I came out to see about that beer you forgot to send me up—"

"Most regrettable, Monsieur—"

"Never mind that. I'm standing in the corridor, ready to come downstairs after my drink, and there was this piece of delight, slinking along the corridor. And she had on a uniform, like your girls wear who tidy the upper floor bedrooms."

"Yes, Monsieur," said Jean, patiently.

"Well, I've never seen her before, and as you know, I've stayed at *The Queen* in the past. So I wondered who she might be? And believe me, Jeanot, old chap, I'd like to know."

"No one, Monsieur," said Jean. "There's no woman works here of that description."

"A guest then?"

"No, Monsieur. We have, at present, no women guests staying at the hotel."

Monsieur of the Beer drew back. He scowled. Then turned on me. "*You* then. If he won't say, *you* tell me. Who is she? I've only spotted her once. But that was enough."

I knew who he must mean, for the one he had detailed was none other than the woman *I* had seen on my first morning, after Madame Cora had grabbed me.

I said, "I don't know who you refer to, Monsieur."

"Oh, is it some shit of a conspiracy? Why? I've had half the other girls in this rat-hole. So why clam up over this one? Aren't I good enough now? Money not good enough?"

"Please, Monsieur," said Jean, "you are upsetting the other customers."

"Fuck the other customers. Come on, Jeanot. Is she *your* fancy piece? I *doubt* it."

The other denizens of the bar were actually quite enjoying this theatre. But at that instant, Mademoiselle Octopus, who had been absent from the room, sailed in at the doors. She loomed over the Beer Monsieur and said, in a scratchy cruel little voice, "Where are your manners? Where do you think this is? Have I to have you ejected?"

And to my amazement, the riotous Monsieur Beer subsided, blushing and begging her for leniency.

At that moment too a flock of would-be drinkers entered from the street, their shoes and boots thick to the ankle in white. As I hurried to serve them I thought, with vague wonder, *Black Eyed Susan doesn't exist — yet two of us have seen her. She must be a ghost.*

Obviously it was unreasonable that I should call her Susan. But I'd lived, even then, in England long enough a while, the phrase had sprung to my mind.

ESTHER GARBER

Having decided she must be a ghost, I felt I should at least reorganize her name. And so she became Suzanne des Yeux Noires.

That night the Patron of the hotel came into my room. I had just staggered in from work and the night was young, only twelve-thirty this time, for the bar (which operated by some autonomous law regulated only by how many heavy drinkers were present) had closed up early.

"Well, now," said the Patron. "Here I am."

I looked at him, displeased yet neutral.

He said, "Is *this* the dungeon they've given you? Poor little girl. What a nasty sty – and so *cold*. Have you turned the radiator off?"

"It doesn't work," I sullenly told him.

"Dear God. You'll catch pneumonia. Well, well," he rambled on, idling round the room, as if examining my personal clutter and knick-knacks, of which, as I've said, I had few and displayed none. "What was your name again? Estelle, was it?" When I couldn't be bothered to correct him, he cogitated "No, no, that's wrong. Is it Estrellya, then?"

I said, gently, "Monsieur, please excuse me, but I'm very tired. I have to be up before six tomorrow."

"Of course, of course. Well, well," he said. He sat down on the bed, and gradually began to undo his shoes.

In bemused horror I watched this procedure, which was followed soon enough by an unknotting of his tie, a removal of his coat and waistcoat.

All the while he went on speaking.

"No, it's not Estrellya, is it? Estina. That was it? No? No, no. You see, my grandmother still believes I must want young women. She has always thought this, but in fact," he rolled his eyes at the ceiling, from which icicles might well be hanging, "in fact I married young only from duty. My wife died long ago. My mother lived longer, but then she too died. My grandmother still lives, voraciously. Well. So it goes. So it goes."

By now he had divested himself, not only of his previous character, but also of all his clothing aside from his shirt. Bulbous hairy legs, veined like the best marble, protruded beneath, also there sometimes showed the soft beak of his penis, which lay innocently already sleeping. He got up again, pulled wide the bed, and quickly coiled himself into it.

He was entirely asleep in seconds. The room rattled at his baritone snores.

I, like the fool I was, stood there in my dark uniform dress, very like, I thought, that which Suzanne des Yeux Noires had worn, save hers, (despite Monsieur Beer's mention of legs) had seemed rather longer, almost to her slender ankles.

What now?

After ten minutes of standing – my room did not provide a chair – I let myself back out of the door. I poised in the corridor, which was really warmer than my room, though lit only by the snow moon at the window, considering that the dark hairs I'd found on my pillow were really not so very long, and might have belonged to the Patron (the musk of violets being probably only my imagination), and that maybe the man often slept in that bed.

It was odd. But I have met – had met even then – so much oddity.

While I was stuck there in the corridor, wondering if I should now creep down to the kitchen and sleep Cinderellerishly in the grease by the ovens, another door opened far up the passage.

Someone stole out, voluptuously stealthy in her nightgown, her hair undone and lying loose all around her, like a soft silver mist.

"Oh, has that pig gone in your room? What a pig. Come with me. It's freezing out here."

She took me by the hand and led me, in a daze, along the passage and into her own chamber. It was Sylvie.

Ah, what a transformation she'd achieved. Admittedly, her radiator worked, but all else was due to her, or so I guessed. Her bed was heaped with a glorious patchwork quilt, made of rather map-shaped pieces, colored blue and scarlet, amber and ivory. Rugs massed on the floor. Thick curtains of a dense indigo masked the icy unfriendliness of the outer streets, and her overhead lamp, though unlighted, had a shade like a lace birdcage. Meanwhile a stand of candles blazed on a table near the bed, and here too were spread cosmetics, mirrors, sweets, a bottle of wine even, and two polished glasses.

"Do you like my room?" asked Sylvie, like a clever child.

"Very much."

"I've been here three whole months. You have to do something, don't you?" I looked at her in a bedraggled way. Laziness, or some other worse element, tended to make me always feel I had better do nothing. But I nodded. She said, "Let's have a glass of wine. You can share my bed if you like. Look, it's huge. And we're just two little girls, aren't we?"

We had the wine. I'd thought she hadn't liked me. And besides she might turn like milk in the morning. But milk keeps better in winter.

I undressed behind a bird-painted screen she had, and put on one of her nightgowns. I undid my hair. Next we were in the bed, which was warm from her occupancy.

"Shall I blow out the candles?" she said. She looked playful.

"Yes," I said.

In the dark there was a brief pause, during which my blood hummed like a hive of bees. She was less than my hand's length from me.

Then she moved up close to my side.

"We'd better stay together, or we'll be cold."

"Yes."

"What fine hair you have, Esther. Oh dear, so sorry, I never meant to touch you *there*."

"That's all right, Sylvie."

"Oh! There. I've done it again. What will you think?"

"Well, perhaps..."

"Really? Oh!" Now more genuinely, "Oh – that's – wonderful—"

I felt over every inch of her through the nightgown, which presently anyway we took off, and next mine.

She had that smooth deep skin from the south, heavy and satisfying as treacle. Her hands and elbows were rough, but all the rest glided. Her breasts had centers like the smooth pink sweets on the table. I sucked them until I thought they might explode like sherbet bonbons in my mouth, and Sylvie yelped softly, pulling my hair. The core of her tasted of the sea, and had the texture of firm plums. The urge to bite her was nearly unbearable, so I bit her stomach all along its curve, leaving little marks to remind her in the morning. Before returning into the depths of the seaplum.

She wouldn't let me make her come though, not like that. I had to lie over her, pressing her down, staring at her eyes in the dark which it seemed to me was total, thanks to the thick curtains. Our hands twisted and spasmed. At the last glorious seconds she became all I'd ever wanted. But thank God, once we had fallen together like a collapsing fan, silently screaming into each other's flesh, she became again only a charming companion in a bed warm as toast.

"That was lovely," she whispered as we turned over to sleep, spine to spine, her buttocks couched in the small of my back. "And I knew you would."

"How?"

"Just something. You know Madame was like that once? Or so they say."

"Madame – which Madame? Madame Ghoule?"

But Sylvie slept, her appetite appeased for now.

I lay awake about twenty minutes, curious, almost happy.

And long before the sadist battered on the door at a quarter to six, Sylvie and I had woken once more, and once more coupled, twining as if we had slept away our bones.

"Yes, Madame!" called out Sylvie however, at the appalling knock. I of course kept quiet.

And through the door Madame Ghoule declared, "*You* must wake that new one, that Estette. I have been unable. My God, how she snores—"

A delicious time then, after all, at *The Queen*. Sylvie and I. We would meet almost every night when our work was done. I bought her a few flowers and cakes, cheap beads, a comb for her hair, proper tribute, and all I could afford, smuggled in wrappers or under my outdoor coat. The town, still floured with the now-decaying snow, opened up its shops for me. By day she and I would pretend we didn't care for each other much, and sometimes she would say something faintly disparaging about me to one of the others, loud enough I couldn't fail to hear, and then she'd wink at me. At night, between the sessions of sex, she would mock the other girls. I told her to be careful, to be wary.

I didn't love her. It was more enchanting than that.

Love can be a shackle so loaded with its own imprisoning power; it hauls you to the ocean's floor and throttles you there. But this was that other sort of love, honorably ancient as dust, and light as the opening spray of champagne that, once left, soon invisibly dries.

Did I then think of the other one, the ghost, Suzanne? Yes. Now and then. Involved in this unexpected romp, that gave me besides a warm bed, and even demonstrated for me the way to make the hot water come in the bathroom (Sylvie beating with a broom-handle on the tap) that also managed to see me given slices of meat in the kitchen, and other delicacies (by telling the contra-suggestive cook I should on no account get anything of the sort), even so, unforgivably (or inevitably perhaps, if I'm honest), some part of me was still glancing round to find the pain, the elation, of an unrequited obsession, therefore the black-eyed arrogance of Suzanne, the ghost.

To that end, I began to seek out Madame Cora, the grandmother of the peculiar Patron.

After all, that first morning, it was she who had yanked me up into the corridor where I'd seen Suzanne. And surely, if Monsieur Beer had beheld the apparition too, Madame Cora must likewise have done so. (To approach Monsieur himself had been out of the question. Following his outburst in the bar and the Octopus intervention, he'd fled the hotel the next day.)

Madame Cora, though, was a handier proposition. She dined almost every evening at eight o'clock in the dining room, where I was by now nearly always expected to assist in the service of guests.

Normally the Chief Waiter tended to Madame Cora, but once I had made up my mind, which took, I admit, two or three weeks, I slipped between them like a narrow knife.

"Good evening, Madame. We have an excellent fish tonight."

"What do you say?"

"An excellent fish. The cook has prepared it carefully and several people are praising it. I hope you'll like it, Madame. May I bring you a fresh carafe of water? This one has a fly in it."

She stared into the carafe, which had nothing in it but the water. She said, "Very well. What's your name?"

"Esther, Madame. We met on my first day at the hotel."

"Est," she said, looking at her first course, a sort of mushroom creation, which she'd broken but not eaten. "The East."

The Chief Waiter was there. He leaned over us. To me he said, "What are you doing here? Table seven wishes the roast chicken with sauce."

"Excuse me. Madame's water has a fly in it."

"A fly? In winter? Never. There's no fly."

"Please look there. It's a fly."

He raised the carafe, squinting in, his large, hopeless, unfair eyes expanding through the glass into a pair of ghastly swimming eye-fish.

"Nothing," he said.

But Madame Cora flew into a temper. "Let her take it away. There's a fly! Of course! Do as you're told."

He cowered and I sped out with the decanter.

Coming back in after a moment with, of course, the same water, I saw Madame Cora was now sitting alone again, the Chief Waiter spun off like a displaced molecule to the other side of the restaurant.

When I set the carafe back down before her, she put out her hard and bony hand and gripped my wrist, as at our meeting. This time I bent willingly towards her.

"Did he have you?" she asked in a low rasping voice.

She meant the Patron.

I said, truthfully, "He spent a night in my bed, Madame."

"Ah, good, good." She nodded and let me go. "He must be appeased," she said, obscurely. Her old eyes – what was she – seventy, seventy-five? – were dark yet filmed over. Her sad and disappointed lips turned down. And yet there was to them, those lips, something that once had been gallant – the lines running upward before the depression of gravity and age pushed them earthward. "He may wish to do it again," she said. She shot me a look.

"Very well, Madame," I said, meekly.

"Good. You're a good girl."

I filled her water glass. She seemed thoughtful. I said, "Madame, that young woman who passed us that day in the corridor, she had brown hair and very black eyes. Who is she?"

Madame Cora glanced at me again, and she smiled, pressing her sad mouth upwards.

"So you *saw* her?"

I straightened. A chill ran over my back.

"Yes. I did. What – who – is she?"

Her smile closed like a secret lock. She said, still locked smiling, "I don't want the fish. Bring me some cake now, and cheese."

She saw my defeat. She seemed to take definite pleasure in it. I understood it would be currently useless to try to question her further. Even so I said, "I call her Suzanne."

"Do you?" she asked. She laughed. It was a spiteful little bark, like her grandson's, the Patron. "Suzanne? That was never her name."

She must have made some gesture to him, for the Chief Waiter was suddenly there again, hustling me aside. "Go back to the kitchen at once! What are you at, bothering Madame?"

And back to the kitchen I went.

That night, in bed with Sylvie, I let her feed me chocolate, and told her I was unhappy as I'd been thinking of my dead mother, and my father, who was a crook. This launched her into some long epic tale of her own family and its vices, and in the end I was able to avoid making love with her. That night I felt I couldn't. But in the early hours of morning, before the yammer of Madame Ghoule on the door, I seized Sylvie in my arms, waking her to sensation so violently and harshly she began to cry, though her weeping was soon lost in other passions. "You're so unkind, Esther," she told me, snuggling into my body afterwards. "Don't you like me, really?" "I think you're quite wonderful," I said. "No," she said. "But never mind. Do you know," she went on, as I was drifting off again to sleep, "who gives me these chocolates, and the wine?" "The Patron," I suggested dreamily, She giggled. She said, "Oh no, it's..." I was asleep before I heard what she said.

I dreamed I was standing by a vast expanse of water, brown and glowing, a river. Palm trees rose above me, with pleated tines like sculpted bronze. A crocodile waddled like a green sausage on legs across a mud bank, and I heard my mother's long-ago, exasperated sigh.

When I woke up, in the moments before her knocking, I thought, *It's Madame Ghoule who is this way too, and who accordingly gives Sylvie confectionary and wine.* And when the knocking came and Sylvie only stirred in my arms, I called out loudly, "Thank you, Madame. We are awake."

To her credit I heard her answer steadily, "Excellent. Please see you're both downstairs and at work in twenty minutes. "

The snow which had loosened and regrouped, now sagged, and turned to a thick dirty sorbet, that ran off the town, leaving the roofs with loud bangs like the concussion of bombs. Released, the trees lifted black arms to a wet sun, against a scudding sky. Soon feathers of new life appeared on them, a tawny northern fuzz that, in a handful more weeks, might break to pale green.

Standing in the bathroom in my slip, hammering as usual on the hot tap, I watched in astonishment as the entire faucet gave way, spewing out fairly hot water across most of the room.

By the time I'd summoned assistance, the bathroom was flooded, the water, now growing cool, spooling away down the corridor in a glowing river.

Madame Ghoule summoned me.

"This is a disgrace, Mademoiselle."

"I'm sorry, Madame."

"Sorry is no use. Do you know how much it will cost to repair the damage?"

"No, Madame."

I thought she would dock my already meager wages. Instead she proclaimed, "We haven't been at all satisfied with your work, besides. You're slapdash, tardy, off-hand with the customers and, I hear, leave bits of food stuck on the plates when you wash them." I could say nothing to that. It was all true. "The cook has said you eat too much. In addition, you were told you're allowed only one bath a week, yet I gather you've been bathing almost every day." Also undeniable. I thought to myself, Yes, and you're jealous that I get into bed with Sylvie. But Madame Ghoule didn't list that among her sequence of complaints, of which there were several more. When she concluded, I waited for the axe to fall. It fell. "I think we shall wish to dispense with your services. Indeed, I think we shall be overjoyed to dispense with them."

Spring was coming. Despite my small gifts to Sylvie, and various essentials I'd had to buy for myself, I had by now accumulated enough to tide me over. I had been at the hotel called *The Queen* for almost two slow months – I would have been off anyway before much longer.

"Very well, Madame. Can I expect any wages owing to me?"

"Certainly not. Think yourself lucky you'll be asked to contribute nothing to the repair of the bathroom and corridor. "

There are few things so liberating, I've found, as being summarily sacked. Not even any guilt attaches.

I went straight upstairs to my cold room (noting in passing, the Patron had been in my neglected bed again, this time smothering the pillow with hair oil), and changed into my own clothes and high-heeled shoes. I brushed my hair and left it loose on my shoulders, and applied my reddest lipstick to my mouth.

Then I went straight down to the bar.

"What are you doing here like that?" demanded Jean, caught, I could see, between abruptly noticing me as female, and prudish slavish disapproval. "You can't wear all that rouge, or those shoes – and some drunk's sure to spill something on that dress."

"I've been fired," I announced. "I'll have a cognac. Here," and I slid the coins to him across the counter.

Bewildered by this painted fiend, who only an hour ago had been meekly pouring out alcohol or coffee beside him, Jean measured my drink and handed it to me. Behind me, I heard a dim stirring and rustle, as Mademoiselle Octopus laid down her sewing in the kiosk.

"I want to know something, Jean," I said, boldly. "That dark woman the beery Monsieur liked upstairs – who is she?" He blinked, and I went on, "I know there *was* someone, though you were at such pains to deny it. I did too, remember, to help you out. But now I'd like to be told."

Jean opened his mouth. Stubbornly closed it. Then took a breath and said, "It's none of your concern."

"Did I say it was? I just want to know."

"Oh," said Jean, also abandoning any reserves of the commonplace, "I know why *you'd* want to know. Oh yes. I've heard about your sort of girl. Oh yes. Sylvie's said to all of us, she's not safe when you're around. Had to lock her bedroom door, she said, you were so persistent."

I shouldn't have been startled by betrayal. Being betrayed, one way or another, had become symptomatic of my existence. But for an instant my guts gave a sick lurch, and I downed the cognac, and thrust the empty glass back at him. "Another. And watch your tongue, sonny. It's Sylvie you should be careful of. And that Ghoule. Also your Patron. This hotel is a madhouse."

Jean wouldn't refill my glass, so I grabbed the bottle from him, and sloshed two glasses full. Clattering down more coins I said, "Drink up, before the sewing witch comes over."

Sheepishly, used I suppose, as many of them seemed to be, here, to being overridden by women, Jean swallowed his glass-full.

He said, to the counter, "You'd better not go after that woman upstairs, though. Just better not. Not if you've been entertaining the Patron."

Unnatural woman and *also* floozy, it seemed.

"Why is that?"

"She's his regular. Class. Brown hair and black eyes and that swarthy skin from the south. That's her. He makes her dress like a chambermaid in one of the old uniforms. We all *know*. We keep quiet."

A dank disappointment listed through me. One more betrayal. For my mystic Suzanne of the Black Eyes was not a ghost, only some upstairs classy whorey convenience of the hotel owner's, of whom we must all pretend unawareness.

"I don't believe you," I said, casually. "How could you know anything about what the Patron does?"

"Well, that's where you're wrong, see. I do know. She's the widow of a living man. He's crippled, and they've fallen on bad times. Not a servant in the house. Also she can't get anything from him, in *that* way. So she comes up to visit the Patron now and then. Her name's Henriette de Vallier."

"What an invented-sounding name."

"It's not. It's her name. She lives in one of the rich houses on the rue Rassolin."

A presence was at my shoulder, breathing on me a camphor-flavored pastille. Mademoiselle Coudeban, seamstress of bags for octopuses.

"What is happening? Why is this girl here dressed in this sluttish manner? Go up at once, girl, and wash your face. "

I turned and beamed at her. "Can I buy you a drink, Mademoiselle?"

"What effrontery! It's forbidden to drink on duty in the hotel. As for you, Jeanot, I quite plainly saw you swallow a glass of brandy."

"I gave it him for the shock," I said. "I'm no longer the employee of this strange building. I can do as I please."

"And I, miss," snapped Mademoiselle Octopus, "can have you put straight out of the door."

Although she had set down her sewing, I could see it over her shoulder, lying across the chair arm in the open kiosk. It was a shape like a map of India, perhaps, and of a deep amber color. I had seen such shapes and shades in the patchwork coverlet of my lover Sylvie. Suddenly I knew quite well who else had given Sylvie presents for her favors, and who else, too, had been betrayed. In that instance, to me.

I didn't have to say a word. By some bizarre osmosis of our brains, Mademoiselle Coudeban and I immediately and completely understood each other, and that, for now, I was potentially the more dangerous.

Her thin crunched-together face turned bitter and pale like a sour fruit sucking on a sour fruit.

I said, "Won't you take a drink with me, Mademoiselle?"

"It isn't allowed. But for yourself, since you say we no longer employ you – well. You must do as you like."

After my earlier onslaught on Madame Cora in the dining room, I'd done nothing else, not knowing what else I could do.

Sometimes I had, during my breaks or on some excuse, gone up to the top corridor and walked about, passing several doors unmarked, or marked *Private*, but no longer knocking. In fact at that juncture no one at all seemed to be on the top floor. The hotel guests were, all told, very scarce; one came across them only in the bar or restaurant, or very occasionally on the stairs between the second and third stories. I'd already arrived at a surreal conclusion, which was that the hotel was primarily run only in order that its own weird, deviant and deranged life might go on. The enlisting of guests – even staff – being simply camouflage.

Now I'd been manumitted from slavery to the organism, however, I stalked out into the town, warmed by the brandy, and set off towards the street Jean had stipulated. I had seen it before, gone down it once on one of my solitary, aimless walks, which only gained meaning after I began to buy gifts for the faithless Sylvie.

The houses were tall and joined, with sloping ridged pestles of roofs. Iron railings enclosed clipped cold gardens the snow had spoiled, and here and there was a courtyard, one now with a little horse standing alone in it, browsing at a tub of wintry grass. Few cars moved along the avenue.

As in the hotel's upper corridor, I went to doors and knocked. Generally a maid appeared. "Oh, excuse my troubling you. But I've lost my kitten. Have you seen it? A little ginger cat, tiny—" Some were sentimentally concerned and took up my time suggesting various means to recapture the errant feline. Some gave me a gimlet glance and saw me off with a "No, Mademoiselle. You must try elsewhere." But all managed to inform me, in roundabout ways they never noted, that theirs was not the house of Madame de Vallier.

At the fifth house along the right-hand side, where a bare peach espalier clawed at the wall, a woman answered the door who wasn't a maid.

I looked at her, her fair hair held back by clips, her white face, green eyes and narrow mouth. No Black Eyed Susan she.

"Your kitten? Well, Mademoiselle, how can you have been so careless as to lose it?"

"Oh come, Lise. Don't be harsh." This from the shadowy stair along the hall. The voice was low and eloquent, and then there came the faintest slenderest gust of violets—

I stepped back, my heart hammering like the broom-handle on the tap of my ribs, to disrupt them and let hot hope explode outwards, splashing the espalier, the blonde woman, and anything else within reach.

Why do I put myself into such positions? Quivering down some alien street, knocking at doors and lying, in case I might find the barbed blade of a perfect, dreadsome love—

Then she was in view, the second woman who had spoken.

I said, before I could prevent it, "Madame de Vallier!"

"Oh, yes," she said. "Do you know me?"

"Forgive me, Madame. Not at all. I saw you – in a shop in the town, and someone spoke your name."

"How odd," she remarked.

She stood looking at me, not five feet away, the other woman, who she had called Lise, eclipsed and slunk aside.

Madame de Vallier paused in thought. Then: "Now the best thing," Madame de Vallier said, deciding on being firm and kind, "if the little cat has a favorite food—"

As she proceeded to give me her good-natured advice, I gazed at her, dumbfounded. Here was the woman with whom the Patron slept, presumably sometimes even in the beds of hotel staff such as myself. And she was exactly as Monsieur Beer had described her. Her chestnut brown hair was strictly tied back into a snood of black velvet. Her honey skin and faultless figure encased in neat black clothes that did indeed additionally reveal slim and well-formed legs. She was apparently in sartorial mourning for the living man of whom she was a 'widow.' The man who couldn't give her any more sex, or servants. She was pretty, certainly, in a pre-cast, unsurprising way. And her eyes were the dark brown of damp cedar wood. But not black, not black at all. Nor was she Suzanne. That is, she wasn't, nor could I ever have mistaken her for, the black-eyed creature I'd glimpsed in the corridor during my first hour at the hotel. Monsieur Beer and I, evidently, had seen two different women.

Henriette de Vallier finished her treatise on cat-retrieval. I thanked her effusively, and paced back down the path, looking as dispirited as any girl might who had just mislaid her beloved kitten. (I heard Lise malignly whisper, "She'd been drinking, too. You could smell it on her.")

I went and sat under a plane tree in the Place de la Fontaine, which was fountainless and winter-grim.

The life of the town mechanically passed me, up and down. Everyone was so involved, slotted each into their niche, whether comfortable or not, with a kind of self-satisfied assurance. *I am angry, so angry,* would say one face going by, or another, *I am in such a hurry,* or *I am lost in my thoughts – ask me nothing.* Even the smaller children who appeared seemed already enlisted in this army of the predestined, and already in the correct uniform and with the correct rank ascribed.

Only I sat there, outlawed flotsam – or jetsam more likely, hurled from the floating insane asylum called the Hôtel Reine.

I don't believe in ghosts, or think I don't. Or didn't or thought I didn't, then.

But I *had* seen her. She *had* gone by. And if the delicate whiff of violets was only some leftover of the other presence of Madame de Vallier, Black Eyed Susan had still been as real as I, or as the dotty old Cora, hanging on my arm.

Which brought me again, of course, to the Patron's grandmother. For she alone had been with me, when that being crossed our path. And she alone had later said to me, "So you *saw* her," and "Suzanne? That was never her name."

That night I dined in the restaurant of the *Queen Hotel.*

I wore my one reasonable dress, which really *was* quite reasonable. I had an omelet, a salad, and something that may have been pork. Also a bottle of wine.

I was scrutinized by everyone, both the waiters and the customers, who all knew me by now as "That one, that Esette."

At ten minutes to eight, Madame Cora came in, leaning slightly sideways, as if on an unseen companion, and so moving rather like a crab. She sat down at her usual table, and the Chief Waiter hastened to her side. As always happened she took a long while, questioning every dish, clicking her tongue over the cook's efforts, asking for water, saying her napkin was soiled.

They brought her a plate of eggs, and she played with it, testing it as someone does who is perhaps searching for poison. When she laid down her fork, she looked around at last. And her watery grey-black eyes alighted on me.

Rather than seem amazed, Madame Cora nodded, as if I were a somewhat inferior acquaintance of long-standing. I picked up my glass of wine, and went across to her table, hearing about me the dismayed murmurs of our fellow diners.

"Oh, sit down, sit down," she said impatiently. And down I sat. "What do you think is in this food?"

"Eggs, I believe, Madame."

"Possibly. Useless, this cook. There was one here once, a fine cook. But that was before the war. He died in the trenches," she added, with a frown of selfish annoyance. "Since then, none of them are any good." She was such a little, wizened thing. On her hands there were no rings, not even one for wedlock. She dabbed her lips and pushed the dish away. "Do you want it?"

"No thank you, Madame. I've already eaten."

"Who are you?" she said.

"My name's Esther, Madame."

"Est," she said, as before. "From the East... How old are you?"

"Twenty-eight."

"*Pouf!* You look only sixteen. A girl. If you're so old, you should be married."

"If you say so."

"Don't you like men?" I said nothing, only modestly lowered my eyes. Madame Cora went on, "I never did. Foul brutes. But there, I had no choice. I used to bribe him, my husband, bring him girls – it kept him away from me. Then, despite everything, I had a child. My God, my God, the agony. They gave it to me and crowed, 'Look. A son.' I hated it at once. It grew up to be the present Patron's father, you see. Then there was *this* one, the Patron himself. I've brought them all women. It's all they can think of, pushing themselves into some woman. Horrible, stupid. What can it all mean? The church says it's our duty. But no, no, that was then. Surely that's all changed by now."

Did she want an answer? She'd fixed her eyes on me, drawing mine up to meet them. "I'm afraid it hasn't changed," I said.

"No. Of course not. Have you borne children?"

"No," I said

"You've been lucky."

"Yes."

The Chief Waiter had reached her table again, and he said to her sternly, "Is this person pestering you, Madame?"

"Pester? *You* are the one pesters me." She flapped the clean 'soiled' napkin at him. "Be off! Where's my fruit? I wished for fruit. The Patron shall hear how casually I'm treated here." The Chief Waiter bowed and left us. Obviously he was accustomed to her ways. "I sent you to my grandson, didn't I?" she asked me. When I nodded, she said, "I hope you'll forgive that. I suppose he never gave you any sort of remuneration. No? That's like him. They say he keeps a mistress in the rue Rassolin, but how can one credit that? Even so, he lavishes a lot of money somehow, and none here. This wretched place," she waved her little wooden hand at the whole room, "it's falling apart. Nothing spent on it for years. Do you know, today one of the bathrooms exploded? What a thing. The taps blew off under the pressure of the water. Then the water soaked into the passage and through into the rooms below. Thousands of francs will be needed. I tell you, little girl," she said, conspiratorial, "one more good winter snow, and the whole crumbling edifice will collapse in rubble on the street."

I had the instant image of the hotel performing this very act. Clouds of dust and snow-spray rose into a black sky speckled with watching stars; bricks and pieces of iron bowled along the road.

And suddenly, as if she saw this image too, she gave some of her sharp little barks of laughter.

"Don't think," she said, "I'd be sorry. Not even if a ceiling dropped on my head. Oh, I hate it here," she said. And as suddenly as the laughter, her eyes were luminous and nearly youthful with tears. I had the urge to take her wooden hand. I didn't risk it. "I was young once," she confided. "Do you believe me?"

I said, "We were all young once, Madame."

"*Pouf!* You're a baby still. Twenty-eight – what's that? I was in my thirties, and still young. Oh yes. *That* was my time. Oh, the naughty things I did. He never knew, my son, and my husband was dead by then, thank God. Well, it wasn't any of their business. I worked here for them both, their skivvy. But it had many benefits, that. I would get to meet all the guests, enter their rooms even, quite intimately. There was always some excuse. Yes, little one. You and I might have had some fun then."

I looked at her narrowly. Now her eyes were sly.

I said, "I'm sure we'd have got on famously."

"*Famously!* Oh you English. Yes, I can hear that you are, all right, even through your French which is so exactly fluent."

Unwisely no doubt I assured her, "In fact, Madame, I'm a Jewess."

"A Jewess. Well then. The Jews are not so popular now, are they."

"If they ever were," I said.

"An arrogant race," she said. "And yes, *you're* an arrogant little thing. Of course you're a Jewess. But I had a lover once, a Jewess."

There. It was out. She had consorted, not so much with a pariah ethnic race, but with her own, that of women.

Her tears, which had dematerialized, shone out in her eyes again, and I thought she would reminisce now over past love. But she said again, pathetically, stoically and hopelessly, "How I hate it here." And she didn't mean, I saw, only the hotel. It was the world she hated, and what she had become in it. *Here* meant also her flesh.

Just then a waiter, attended by his Chief, came to the table with a long dish of offal-stuffed sausages.

"No!" snapped Madame Cora. "Take it away. I will have fruit."

"Madame – it's winter. There are only the apple tarts and the pears in syrup."

"Bring me the pears. They will be disgusting, but it's all I can expect, now."

The two waiters went away, bearing the sausages before them.

It wasn't that she bored me. But the pressure of her sorrows (like water on the riven tap), was very great, even overwhelming. Any plan I'd had, gradually to lead her to the elusive subject of the woman I called Suzanne, had drained from me as she spoke of her life. What was this momentary spark to that bleak digression? And anyway, did I really care? 'Suzanne' perhaps had only been another of my means to kill time at the hotel. In addition, I had begun to be alarmed someone might soon summon me again to Madame Ghoule, who would then demand, since I could afford to buy myself brandy, and had dined in the restaurant, that after all I pay over all my accrued money towards the repair of the water-damage. It seemed, did it not, so much more ruinous than I'd thought.

Because of all this, I was shifting mentally, thinking up a polite reason to leave Madame Cora, and so make my escape from the hotel. And in that way, I almost missed the next abrupt change in her eyes.

When I defined what was happening, I was caught a moment longer, staring. It was as if a sort of glittering shutter fell through her eyes, first opening them wide as windows, and then closing them fast behind itself, so only that steely, glittering façade was left behind.

She sat bolt upright, her chin on her hand, these metallic and non-human eyes fixed on something behind me.

I turned round.

And all across the dining area, I saw a slim woman dressed in elongated black that was not a uniform, a large black hat with a silvery feather in it perched on her dark hair. She was in the process of walking out of the room. And yet – I hadn't seen her in the restaurant until that second. (Had she perhaps entered behind my back, while the old woman and I were talking?) Whatever else, I knew her at once. It was She from the corridor. Not Henriette de Vallier, but Black Eyed Susan.

"Pardon me, Madame—" I stuttered, rising, throwing back my chair. Madame Cora's face seemed to dress itself in a kind of leer. She found my urgency funny, of course. She knew *precisely* what I was at.

In the doorway I brushed hastily past Jean, who was coming in with a tray of drinks. He cursed me, but I scarcely noticed.

Black Eyed Susan – Suzanne des Yeux Noires – was crossing the lobby, going under the yellow electric lamp, exiting into the blowy crystal vistas of the night.

As I too dashed out on the pavement, I was glad the snow was long gone. For already *she* was far ahead of me, walking swiftly in her little high-heels, that gave at each step a flash of ankle in a clock-patterned stocking. The wind blew her hat-plume to a ripple like a sea-wave in storm.

I could smell the unborn spring, acid as new wine, tossed by the wind. I could smell a hint of musk and violet – as unlike the scent of Madame de Vallier, or the Patron's hair oil, as any perfume could be that came from the same flower.

Now I was running. Dare I call out? What would I call? Suzanne! Suzanne! Wait just one instant—

But Cora had told me anyway, Suzanne wasn't her name.

At the street's corner, under a lamp, she turned, my quarry. She looked back at me, or I thought she did. All across the distance, in the web of light, her two space-black eyes, gleaming like frost on a steely surface. Then she was around the corner.

I ran to it, and reached it in seconds. But she had disappeared.

I patrolled up and down the street a while, looking in at doorways, up at windows, lighted or un, once into a lively café.

She must live, or visit, in this street. Perhaps I should knock on doors? I didn't knock. I wandered only up and down, until a man came out of the café and offered me a drink, and I had to tell him I was waiting for my friend. "He hasn't turned up, has he?" said the man, triumphant. "Why not give me a try?" But I told him I feared my friend was ill and I must go to him, and hurried away back to the hotel.

Even from outside I saw some fresh kind of uproar was going on, the lobby full of muddled figures and someone shouting for something, I couldn't make out what.

I entered, and stood at the edge of the crowd, and Jean thrust out of it, pasty-faced, and slouched past me, though the street door and away up the street. Also I heard the telephone being used, clacking like a pair of knitting needles, and Madame Ghoule's guttural, "No, he must come. At once, if you please. This is Madame Ghoule at *La Reine*. Please make haste."

And then the entire unintelligibly chattery crowd was falling silent, and down the stairs, and into the crowd, parting it like the Red Sea, came the Patron, greasy grey, his spectacles in his hand, and looking ashamed, as if caught out in some particularly socially-unacceptable crime.

"Make way, it's the Patron." "Let him by, poor fellow."

He went on into the restaurant. And the crowd stole after him, Madame Ghoule lunging among them, crying out now in a clarion tone, "The doctor's on his way, but his car has broken down. He'll have to walk."

In the big room though, the crowd, composed only of a scurry of waiters, a selection of guests and customers from the bar, spread itself, and showed its essential thinness. A couple of people were still seated at their tables, they too looking more embarrassed and depressed than anything. Altogether it was a badly attended show, the audience not large enough, nor moved enough, to honor the tragedy.

Which tragedy then? Oh, that of Madame Cora, who, sitting at her table with her chin propped on her hard little hand, and her eyes wide open, had died in their midst without a sound.

No one had noticed, it seemed, until the Chief Waiter brought her the pears in syrup.

She must have finished that very moment I got up to run after the phantasmal Suzanne. What I'd seen occur in Cora's eyes was then after all truly an opening, and a closing. But the almost sneering amusement on her face had only been death.

It seemed she hadn't suffered. A massive apoplexy, the doctor assured everyone. Congratulating, very nearly, the indifferent Cora on such a textbook exodus. It would have been too quick for pain, he said. This I believed. Nor had she wanted to stay. If the ceiling had fallen on her, she said...Well. It had.

I packed my bags that night, unmolested, and left. I was only astounded to meet Jasmine the chambermaid in a corridor, who said to me fiercely, "Fancy going with a slut like that Sylvie. I'd have liked to be your friend. And I can keep my trap shut about things."

Surprises everywhere.

I took the train to the city, and found a room. As I was always doing. At least in this lodging I was allowed to make a fire, and the landlady offered hot coffee and bread in the mornings.

Of course, I had completely given up my search for, my pursuit of, Black Eyed Susan.

Perhaps I should invent an epilogue, in which I disclose that, before leaving the hotel, I'd found an old photograph of Madame Cora, and seen at once, with a shock so terrific I staggered, that she was the exact double of my 'Suzanne.'

And demonstrably therefore had *been* 'Suzanne' in her youth. Hadn't she said, Madame Cora, that she longed for her youth, and her female lovers? Hadn't she said that 'Suzanne' was never known by that name?

Maybe it was her ghost I saw, that is, the premonition of the ghost of Cora's past, or even her spatial spirit, finally eluding the hotel and the world and the old wizened body, clad in what Cora thought her own perfect form and age, about thirty, dark and sensuous, *carnal* in her black of mourning for a husband, in that expedient, safely deceased; ready for more adventures in some other place.

Or maybe the woman I saw, for see her – *scented* her – I definitely did, if only twice, was another secret mistress of the unusual Patron. Or even some figment of my own winter madness, which Cora recognized as such, knowing that any woman like Esther must be strange in other ways.

I think of her sometimes – of them both. Black Eyed Susan, vanishing into thin air at two turning points, a corridor, a street corner. Madame Cora vanishing also into thin air, leaving only her husk behind her leering in victory at her last laugh.

THE KISS

Esther Garber

One evening in the provinces, the great actress known as Lalage emerged from a brightly-lit stage door on to the street.

As usual she was treated, as already she had been in the theatre, to a round of tumultuous applause. The venue, the Théâtre des Arches, seldom boasted such stars. But Lalage, of course, by this era, was just beginning to fade a little from her glittering status.

Still beautiful, stately, dressed in slimming black with purple trimmings and mauve gloves, she gazed around her at the admirers, all well-dressed men, who clapped and cheered her. She had that perfect look, part modest astonishment, and part empiric aloofness. She was irresistible.

The men surged forward. They doffed their top-hats, and bowed to her, begging to kiss her hands.

Lalage, and her two bodyguards (tough burly fellows hired by Lalage herself), permitted this.

"Come, come, monsieur," she joked now and then, "you will kiss my hand quite away."

"Would I could *carry* you away, madame. I suppose supper would be—"

"Out of the question? I'm afraid it would."

This scene, like those of the play – a new work by Strindberg, thought fairly shocking – had been repeated over and over in its performance every night. Tonight the play itself had closed however, and Lalage would be borne off by train to the next engagement, which was, she had thankfully remarked, in Paris.

The crowd of male worshippers was drawing back now. Though several, having touched her gloves, lingered at the edges of the light against the backdrop of the darkly lamplit town. They discussed her beauty, even murmured, some of them – the most, or least, observant – on her still-tantalizing maturity, when seen close up.

At this moment a small slight figure came slipping out of the shadows.

Everyone, it seemed, turned in surprise. Here there had been only men, and Lalage, the single woman. But the slight figure was also that of a female. She was poorly and nondescriptly dressed, though clean and not unattractive. In her hands she held a book.

The men, amused, or only fatigued, drew mockingly aside to let her by.

Straight to Lalage the girl went.

"Madame," said the girl in a clear and quite ordinary voice, "madame, I have watched your every performance. I have been transported. May I beg now one extreme favor of you?"

Lalage raised her brows.

"Which is?"

The girl opened the book. It was a copy of the very play the actress had been performing.

"I ask..." said the girl. She was in a curiously-controlled rigor of passion – but this was not immediately obvious. Perhaps Lalage definitely saw it.

"Ask what?" prompted Lalage.

"Ask if you will—" the girl again faltered.

"You wish me to sign the title page?"

"No – no, madame. Not at all. I wish you to *kiss* the title page."

There was a murmur all around. The great crowd of men, assembled like silky black crows in their bourgeois evening finery, were held between ridicule and disapproval. "Good God," they said to each other, "she wants *Lalage* to *kiss* that – *book*—"

But Lalage laughed. "What a strange request."

"It would mean so much to me," said the girl.

Looking up into the eyes of Lalage, the girl turned high her lamp of shining desire. Now Lalage could not fail to see it.

Lalage said, "I wear lip-rouge. I'll ruin the paper."

"I know you wear lip-rouge, madame. That is why I want so badly for your kiss to be imprinted there." Softly, but not so softly some others did not hear, the girl confided, "Another mouth than yours, madame, will be applied to that rose-red kiss, over and over. I promise you that. And though it can, naturally, mean nothing to you, to the one who kisses your kiss, it will mean very much."

Lalage found herself, to her startlement, outgunned, as if by some other greater actor. Generous in her way, Lalage was more taken by this than offended. (It would be ten more years before, her looks and her youth all gone, Lalage would learn how to be bitterly envious.)

She received the book from the girl's slim, mittened hands, and bending, set her kiss like a heavenly bow there on the upturned page.

A kind of wind blew round the street. An ill wind that was composed of several tens of men breathing outward in affront.

Lalage handed the book to the girl, who stood there holding it open like an opened heart. She began to thank the actress, but in that instant, flawlessly as ever sensing the exact timing of her exit, Lalage had turned, and the two minders swept her across the road into her carriage.

The night parted with a clatter of horses' hoofs. The stage door banged shut.

Alone now, the young girl who had dared ask for the kiss, alone among the lamplit shadows and a massed flock of affronted, wolverine-like silk crows.

Some only glared at her. Others plainly felt more active. They circled in on her. All at once she was surrounded.

And only then did she seem to see, the girl (who could not have been more than sixteen years of age), her predicament.

"Well," said one of the encircling enemy, "I think she'd better explain herself."

"Yes, she should. Flouncing about here so late, and no one to accompany her. We might take her for a street woman."

"No doubt she's precisely that. Who else among the fair sex would be so bold."

"No, she's no whore," said another, coming over. He was a bigger, darker man, his cloak and hat of better quality, a gaudy, bruised-looking ring on his finger. "I tell you what *she* is. She's an unnatural woman."

"It's Clavier, the importer," muttered the men. Clavier was respected in the town.

And at his heels, therefore, any who had hung back now approached. Like a dark sand they slid into place all about her, the young girl still holding her open book like a heart.

Spotlit now by some surreal, non-apparent footlight, she stood at the centre of the dark circling circle. Her eyes were down. She did not move.

"I tell you," said Clavier, "I've noted her type before. Sluts who think they are a sort of *man* – and that they can get away with it. And not a decent bone in their perverted little bodies. Good for nothing. You heard her, eh, my men, you heard her, didn't you?" He puffed up bigger, an erection of stern anger. "*Another mouth than yours,*" he aped her loudly, if inaccurately, so all might hear, "*pressed over and over to your kiss.*"

"What a bitch," someone said.

"She deserves anything we might do to her," said another.

"Filthy little creature."

Clavier pressed right in and stood large over the poor young girl.

"You should be punished," he said. "And who would care if you were?"

At that the girl raised her eyes. They were luminous and met his with a wild abandon.

"*One* would care," she cried.

"And who's that?" asked Clavier, settling himself, his hairy ringed hands already flexing to seize either her book or her flesh.

"My father," said the girl. She spoke now clear as a bell.

"Her *father*! Her father would thank us, I believe, for ridding him of this horror."

But Clavier's small eyes had been caught by the girl's eyes. He was thinking all manner of thoughts about her now, and mostly with his body.

She said, "My father, monsieur, is very sick. My father, monsieur, is dying."

"Of shame, no doubt, at having such a dirty daughter."

"No, monsieur. He is dying of old age and hard work and poverty. The doctor has told me, in three days or less, my father that I love so, the only man I ever have loved, will be dead."

"Oh dear," derided Clavier.

But now another man laid his hand on Clavier's arm. "Let her go on." After all, the young girl had spoken of love and loyalty to a man. Yes, let her go on.

"Why else," said the girl, defiant, throwing back her head to look at them all, "do you think I found the courage to come to this theatre night after night, not understanding a word of the play and shocked by it, enduring too insults from men on every side, only to watch the great actress Lalage? It was for my father, gentlemen. My father loves her so. And he was too ill to come, so I came, each night, and each night I went home from the theatre, and described to him every move and gesture of Lalage. Oh, if you could have seen his poor sick sad face light up like a warm window with joy – just from hearing of her."

"Clavier," said the man who had touched his arm, "we have made a mistake here."

The girl said, with arrogance now, proudly and fiercely, "And for whom now do you think I asked that kiss? Whose poor dying lips are they that will be applied to that kiss, over and over? *It is for my father.*"

"Dear God," said Clavier. He had gone pale, seeing he had not only made an ass of himself, but also done himself, even business-wise perhaps, quite a bit of harm.

The other man declared, "Mademoiselle, we owe you a thousand apologies. You are brave and good, one in a million, mademoiselle. Is there any man here would not value such a loyal and magnificent daughter?"

They acquiesced, bowing their heads now, humbled.

For she was a proper woman, as God had made her, putting their sex before her own, serving her father despite her own timidity. What a wife she would make – what a mistress.

Clavier said, "Let me find you a cab, mademoiselle, to see you safe home."

She cast him a look, the virtuous girl. "Thank you. I will not accept anything from you."

They drew sheepishly aside to let her by. Deeply embarrassed, horrified. Not one of them would not draw parallels thereafter among his own female kin. Not one would not be dissatisfied with himself. As for Clavier, two months more and he would leave the town and go abroad. So much for him.

To help her father. She had risked it all. In pure and sweet and proper love. Their champion, and they had tried to dishonor her. For shame!

She ran, heart throbbing, blood bounding, the girl, all the way back to the ramshackle tenement where she lived.

Flying up the stairs, she flung wide the door.

Dancing, she spun about the mean little room, holding out the book.

No father raised his feeble hand. There was no father.

Only the girl, bending now in turn, like a drinking snake, to kiss her first hungry, greedy kiss, on the rose-red printing of Lalage.

"I lied."

Youth

Judas Garbah

Love is not idleness
                    —Le Cler.

In a way, this reminds me of one of my sister's stories. I mean Esther, not Anna. In fact I never mentioned my sisters to him – which is odd, perhaps, as I often complain about my sisters to others, especially to strangers. And already I have started to talk about them, Anna, and Esther. So enough of that.

There was a train going, oh, it doesn't matter at all. The important thing was the snow, which had become the world, outside the train. On black lines ruled across this snow, the train was running to its destination, which would take several days and nights. Huge columns of black smoke poured up from the funnel of the black train, and red cinders blew by on the wind of the train. Everything else was the snow, banks and slopes of it rising to a sky the same color, which was a sort of white but not really white at all. Now and then you saw a forest. It seemed to come close to look, then, repulsed or bored, draw away. And there were wolves, but if I tell you there were, you'll say, oh, he would have to put wolves in here. Well, I tell you, they were red wolves. When the train stopped, or slowed, you heard them howling, that unholy and thrilling sound. I never saw them. Perhaps they didn't exist then, only the voices left behind.

I'd been given a berth, but it was an old train. The berth was magnificent, everything set in mahogany, the bed, the wash-stand. It had a Turkish rug, and plum-green curtains at the window. There were oil lamps, each held up by a little naked brass nymph.

The first day and night I lay in the bed-place and slept. It had been tiring for me where I'd been, and I'd had no proper sleep for a week. After that I woke up, and all the rattling of the train had become a part of my bones, and I thought, I won't sleep again for the rest of the journey. Which was more or less correct. I washed, wobblingly shaved, and changed my clothes, then went out and along the swaying rattling corridor to find the dining-car. In some of the sitting-compartments, they had pulled the blinds down. It was about ten in the morning, but I could hear bottles and laughter, and someone singing to a guitar. What dismal fun.

When I reached the dining-car, breakfast was long over, but they were starting on lunch. I suppose if you breakfast at five or six, by ten you might want something.

A huge woman, the mistress of the dining section, came sailing up to me. She was like the Spirit of Eating. Her hair was roped round and round her head, and she had a fat pasty face with stony eyes in it. Once she had been young and beautiful, you glimpsed this girl, coiled up tight inside her like a fossil, asleep for ever.

She took me instantly, without any requests or arguments from me, to a table. She plumped me in, snapped her fingers. At once there was a boy in uniform, who put a bottle of blue vodka before me and a thumb glass.

The Spirit of Eating saluted me. I asked if she spoke French. She said she did, but her "*Ooow, monsew,*" showed me too how she would speak it! Then she heaved away to see to a trickle of other passengers who were wandering in.

The meal began to arrive quickly, but with great slowness between the courses. Rolls and white butter, salt, and bottles of water. Then the wine I had asked for, very yellow and sour. After almost an hour more, a bowl of potato soup. Three quarters of an hour later, pancakes, very heavy. Then eggs. Then a winter salad. All with long intervals. My watch had been broken in the last city, when my lover (Georges), tried to hurl me down the stairs. But a man along the car kept announcing to us all the time. First twelve, then one, then two o'clock.

The Spirit of Eating presided over us all. The timid diners, under her commanding guidance, the vodka, wine and champagne, had become fulsome, and noisy.

Seeing me smoking, she came and presented to me an open box of long, dark cigarettes, with a silver band on each one.

Although I knew I wouldn't sleep again on the train, I by now wanted to go back to my berth. I was worn out from the food, and the landscape; the snow, the forests creeping up and slinking away again.

When I rose, dizzy with alcohol and the lurching of the car, I saw too it was already becoming twilight. The same tint as the wine, the lamps had been lit. It was an afternoon for the mythic nursery fire, some nanny reading a story over a stodgy English tea.

Passing the Spirit of Eating, I bowed, and thanked her.

She smiled. She seemed pleased with me.

Just as I got to the door, between all the tables with their spotted white cloths, a man was going out in front of me. I can only describe it in that way. He was not coming in, yet was suddenly there, although I had not seen him either in the car, or leaving it. Obviously there was nothing uncanny in that. I'd simply not been paying much attention to the passengers, except to wish they'd shut up.

Georges had said to me, after the episode with the stairs, "You'll be straight from my bed into another's. That's all you're worth." As if he were addressing some poor whore from the market alleys. I had been too scared of him at this point to feel either affronted or acknowledging.

"Excuse me," the man in the corridor said, in a peculiarly accented French. Perhaps he guessed – or had overheard my request to the woman.

I said, not in French, to catch him out, "Take your time, please."

What he had been doing was pausing, just into the corridor, to light one of the dark cigarettes the Spirit of Eating had awarded.

He wore a greatcoat, rather like mine – the train was not warm. His had a collar of lush fur. He was slim, might even be thin inside the coat. His manicured hands were expensive but ringless. His blond hair was as luxurious as the fur and also, like the fur, rather long. He had those eyes, a type of grey, the kind one wants to lick to bring out their color more, though it's already enough. The nose, and bones, were aristocratic, and the mouth savage. A mouth not to be shared with anyone. So you wanted the damn thing.

Outside from the nothingness of the snow, wolves howled even over the train's rattle. But the wolf was on the train.

Now the cigarette was alight, and he lounged back, as if to let me pass. Although I was no fatter than he, the way was narrow and I could only do it by brushing against him. So I brushed.

When I was doing it, he made himself bulkier. Our bodies slid one on another. He said, "Wait, just one moment." Then, "*C'est charmantt.*"

Like the Spirit of Eating, his French was different. I didn't wait, as he said, but moved on. His eyes had blotted their after-image on my sight, like too-bright lamps, and I saw them as I went on down the corridor, floating in front of me.

I unlocked the door of my berth, and went in.

Once there, of course, a madness of boredom rushed over me. I paced the small space. I washed my hands, brushed my teeth. (Anna would have approved.) I leaned at the window glaring at the snow on snow on snow, as the song has it.

I had brought books, but the motion of the train made the print giddy and tiresome. I was drunk, wasn't I? I'd sleep again.

So I lay on the berth bed for an hour and had hallucinations, that is, constant half lapses into sleep when I saw bowls gliding through the air, and once a dark shape like a dog leaping across me.

Someone knocked loudly on my door.

It might be the man to examine the tickets once again, for we had passed a station somewhere and stopped for a second, or half an hour. But I knew it was not he. It was the blond being from the dining-car.

I opened the door. A huge German towered before me, muffled to the lips and eyes in scarves. He had a basket full of chocolate things, beasts in shining paper, boxes of Swiss chocolate flowers.

"Something for journey?"

"Thank you, no."

"You like the chocolate? For present. For lady you love."

"I have no lady I love."

He laughed heartily. "Fine young man like you. Come, come. Buy her this rabbit—"

Squeamishly I saw he would go on bullying until I gave in, so bought the chocolate rabbit, an awful grinning thing. I visualized my lady-love, in little frilly knickers, cruelly biting off the rabbit's ears, and serve the sickly bloody thing right.

But my purchase wasn't enough; it only encouraged him. "Look, look," he burbled, pulling from voluminous inner recesses – his guts for all I knew – reams of silk stockings, and lace gloves.

"Go away," I said. "She doesn't like such things."

"Not like? A lady not like—"

Someone spoke behind the German, in German. I thought the sentence was obscene, but was not sure. The Chocolate German didn't seem angered or distressed. He nodded. *"Jah, jah."* And took himself off, brushing thoroughly past the other who had spoken, so I knew before he was revealed who it would be.

"It seems I rescue you," said the blond wolf.

"Yes. And what are you selling?"

"What would you like?"

"Two days off the journey."

He tipped back his fine head and laughed. He had a throat for strangling, bruising. Irresistible, all of him, probably,

"Let me come in and see your lovely room," he said. I stood there. He said, now in his curious French, "I am in the sitting compartments. I sleep, sitting up, like those dead people, I forget who. And one man sings all night. A wonderful voice. I thought at first, what luck. Now I want to kill him, or make him dumb."

I took some moments after he had ended, going over the French, sorting out what he had really said from its idiosyncrasies. The bastard was informing me he wanted to come in and share my sleeper because he couldn't afford one and was uncomfortable elsewhere. That then, the price.

I handed him the rabbit.

"I bought this for my lady."

"Wouldn't she like it? Oh. But you don't have a lady, surely. Unless they married you off very young."

"Well," I said, "you have the rabbit. Eat the ears first."

"I always," he said coolly, "first bite the head right off, to be merciful."

The look in his grey eyes was like an electric shock. I hoped he wasn't going to do it, eat the rabbit in front of me as he described. The horrible eroticism of it was overwhelming enough, just verbalized.

Of course, I should shut the door. I hadn't, and now, balancing the rabbit lightly, he drew out a bottle of the blue vodka, which I had been told long ago was purified by seething over coals.

"Half an hour," he said. "You might like me."

"I dislike you already."

"How passionate. Splendid."

The train gave a sort of shudder and flung us almost together, then apart. It had slowed suddenly and now stopped.

Through the window in the corridor, I saw we drew into another station. There was no platform, and beyond the wooden buildings, most of which were sheds, the snow went on. It showed such a dearth, such a rift in God's imagination, the snow. He had lost interest, quickly and carelessly spread it, and not bothered to enhance the picture.

By the tracks were the peasants of the region, who had swarthy, cold-blackened faces and hats of fur. They were grouped about a bonfire, which sent up thick smoke, like the stove-pipes of the sheds, and the smoke-stack of the train itself. A flock of geese were in a pen; a cow was being milked, the hot liquid steaming blue.

"Oh, go on," he said.

"What?"

Doors were opening all along the train. I half thought I might get out, for sometimes the train stayed at these halts for an hour. But what was there to see? And already old women were bringing baskets of eggs and loaves and would cluster round me, earth-smelling and jabbering. In one place, on a similar journey, I had had a baby thrust into my arms. Whether this was a plea for money, or they simply wanted me to buy it outright, I didn't know. The guard had come and saved me, shouting, brushing me off. The baby did not cry at all. The poor thing was mauve. What horrible adult half-recalled trauma would all this become in its later years?

Down the corridor now came pushing a band of peasants in a red fug of smell and noise. They carried parcels of chickens and one, another guitar, while granny hobbled behind holding up the family samovar.

The force of this pushed the blond man into me and so both of us back into my compartment.

At once he shut the door, locked it.

"*Mon Dieu, mon Dieu,*" he said. Leaning on the mahogany he undid the vodka bottle. "You have a glass?"

I fetched the toothbrush glass and he filled it to the brim, and handed it back to me.

"To your health."

I swallowed the glassful and he took one directly from the bottle. I knew at once in ten minutes we should be seated on my bed in our shirt-sleeves, passing the bottle between us.

Anna would have said to me, "You must be more careful. For heavens sake, he could have been diseased. Syphilis, TB." Then again she might not. Anna has had times of avid interest in my adventures, all judgment suspended. And Esther...Esther would hardly care either way. While they grew up in starched white little-girl dresses, in a gloomy flat some way above the Nile, I flourished in an Egyptian river-slum. Of course I remember almost nothing about it, since our father withdrew me from it when I was less than five. Again, what adult traumas has it left me? Plenty, I assure you.

The train was only in the station a short while. It left with such abrupt rapidity that, judging by the outcry, certain people were left behind. God knew what would then befall them. Perhaps the locals were, during winter, cannibals.

In any case we were by then sitting on the bed, our coats thrown off because someone stoked the carriage stove and with the vodka we were warm. We passed the bottle to and fro.

He said to call him Stephan – which very likely was not his name. He did not bother to ask my name, calling me instead very quickly by flirtatious pet titles. Finally he leaned across and kissed me on the mouth, while we trembled violently to the motion of the deranged train.

"Do you like this?" he asked, "and...this?"

The sour sodomous ache of lust had the color of darkness. We put it off for hours, and all the light, the peculiar twilight that lasted all afternoon, was gone, when eventually we savaged each other. I had him the first, then he had me. There was a bolt on the door, which I had thought to use. The steward knocked and unlocked in one movement, and finding the door resist, called out. I told him to go away.

About six, Stephan went out while I was lying in a half doze, sore and stupid, too dazed yet to have regrets. He returned with two bottles of champagne. He said dinner would go on until one in the morning. The fat woman had winked at him. Stephan said she knew perfectly well what we were at, and had given him too a handful of the cigarettes. Had I been aware, they had each a grain of opium in them?

He'd wounded me in a dozen places, grazed, blackened and drawn blood. I had done as much for him. He poured champagne down my throat and sat astride me, torturing me with his mouth. I remember his thin white body, with its pristine, faun-like muscles. How his back rippled in the lamplight, his hands gripping me under each arm. He had a canine beauty, though very little body hair. There was something truly terrible about him. The black night beyond the window, frayed now and then with orange cinders, provided an unavoidable motion. The train surged forward, fucking the night on and on. He had the power to make me come, and in the end I resisted him, and still came in long gouging twists of feeling. I began to wish he would go but he showed no need to. Once, as I had him, he muttered a strange phrase in his misleading French: "*Ne que v'on desir.*"

At last we got up, set ourselves to rights, and went to the dining-car together. Our faces were faultless, but under our clothes we hid the bleeding ravages. The Spirit of Eating had sat waiting for us, complacent, like some ancient goddess to whom the male act of congress is especially pleasing. She knew, it was obvious, almost sniffing at us, approvingly, and gliding us to our seats. We were served roast goose, which was reserved for only a few of the diners. The smell was so rich I thought I'd have to leave the car, but the champagne and vodka saw it down. Stephan ordered black bread. It was full of husks. Perhaps he wanted to choke me. There was nothing like opium in the train cigarettes, though they were heady as cigars.

"Shall I come back with you?" he asked.

The Spirit had dipped blackened glasses into sugar and vodka, filled them with vodka, set them alight, and so brought them flaming blue. Stephan swallowed down the flame. Well. He'd already swallowed mine.

"If you want to sleep, take the berth," I said. "I'll stay in the corridor."

"You've had enough of me."

"I've had enough."

"And I can sleep in the bed-place?"

"Please. That's quite all right."

"How generous you are," he said, "you Jews. So scared of us all, you have to placate us."

"If you don't want the bed, don't have it."

"Ah, *petite amande*—"

I blew out the flame and drank the hot vodka, which burnt my lips. We had been cautious in kissing. A nice change after Georges, who was liable to knock out your teeth.

Stephan shrugged. He said the funny little nonsense phrase again. "*Ne que v'on desir.*"

"What?"

He replied, in English now, primly, "I don't want that, my-self."

I must have misheard the French. Or else he misused the lan-guage, saying exactly what he did not mean at all.

"I'm tired," I said.

"But you'd give me the bed. Ah, *mon monstre—*"

I threw a flare of money on the table, enough for the Spirit of Eating, and for him too, if he wanted.

I left the dining-car and went back to my berth. Here I shut, locked and bolted the door. But I knew, when he came and po-litely knocked, I would have to let him in or at least reason with him. The colossal drinking had sobered me, and I wondered if he would now want to slit my throat or scar my face, drinking my blood, then robbing me of anything useful. Georges had spent most of our last days warning me about such people (shades of Anna in her schoolmarmish mode). Once he had tied me up and thrashed me with a piece of rope. But Georges didn't have much stamina. His arms soon ached and I wasn't badly hurt. Then he wept at his weakness, his inability to punish me. Even the strug-gle on the stairs had only harmed my watch.

No one knocked. It was two or three in the morning. I rolled restlessly about on the ruined bed, smelling Stephan's expensive cologne and spent healthy spunk. He had left behind a composite aura of something dangerous, wholesome yet metallic, clean yet impure. I wished he would come back, and dreaded him.

Sleep came, in small unnourishing slices, and I woke fully with a steely dawn. The blind was up, and birds, flying before the sun, threw forward their shadows into the carriage so they seemed to fly straight in and through the wall.

As the train moves, so do the sun, moon and stars. Everything moves. Even the heart. Unavoidable.

But the train wasn't moving. It was static. My bones had so re-corded its rumble and jangle, they played it still. Behind my shut lids, everything sped forward. But no longer.

Some station had occurred again. More cows and pigs and bon-fires and grandmothers.

Yet, even after I'd got up, washed and shaved, dressed myself, the train sat still where it was.

The steward rapped, and called, "Monsieur, monsieur, we are broken up."

I flung wide the door in alarm.

"An accident?"

"Not, not. Snow-bank. Before train, do you see?"

I said that I did. When he was gone, I put on my greatcoat and went out into the corridor, where the door had been left partly open. It was now fearfully cold; I mean it made you afraid. You couldn't think what to do with it. I got out of the train and slid down into a mound of snow to my knees.

On all sides was the nothingness God had lost interest in. Here and there black figures trudged up and down, two or three with primitive lighted torches, whose purpose I couldn't guess. The train was so black and large; it plainly had no place there. You could see this now. Reality must suffer a fatal inanition when plunged among the utterly unreal. Up ahead, a snow slip could be on the line, but that was merely inevitable. It might have dropped straight from that unpainted and undecorated sky. Here there was not even a forest to be seen, let alone a station, a village, a shed. The birds had passed over, but we were immaterial to them.

With a meaty grunt, the Chocolate German thumped into the snow beside me. His basket was empty and his brawn-like, mottled face greasy with desolation.

"We shall be here one week," he announced.

"Indeed."

"Last time it is one week. This time will be one week."

"Really."

"All chocolate sold," he told me with a sinister pride. "They buy it all. Food will run out. And no wood for the stoves. Already all the vodka is drunk."

Oh, yes, I was quite scared. But more of its idea than because I believed it.

Then he lurched malevolently at me, and as I trod quickly back to avoid him, he said, "You had him."

I turned away. The Chocolate German pawed my shoulder. "Let go."

"You had him. We all have had him. He has gone through train like the rodent. Even I. I had him. Never before, I swear. Only woman. Against the wall of a barn in a station, yesterday."

"What are you talking about?"

The Chocolate German took no notice. "He have says he will do it. Makes a list, ticks it off. The first night. Before you get on. Back then. All of us. The peasant rubbish too. Yes, yes, he had them. Last night. They lined up for it, I sold them chocolate as they waited. Their women went to the other end of the carriage not to see. And now he's done, the train has stops."

I lit a cigarette. I was in the land of storytellers. Even Georges had story-told me that. Leaving the Chocolate German where he had sunk in the snow, I walked down the line, passing the mediaeval men with torches.

In the fireman's cabin was a hell of flamelight, but no driver. The enormous muzzle of the train faced out across the waste, up to its stack against a whiteness like a tumbled hill.

Faintly I heard wolves howling over the snow. I thought to myself I had probably actually eaten enough, and drunk it too, to last me a week. That snow could be sucked for fluid. That the German lied about the wood stores on the train.

When I had got back on, I met the steward in the corridor.

"No cause for concern," he said, parrot-fashion, bitterly.

"No, of course," I answered, like a good child.

In the dining-car the Spirit of Eating stood in a black fur coat that swept the ground, directing her uniformed slaves. Seeing me, she came up and said, "We will not starve,

"No, Madame."

There were already rolls and butter laid, the samovar smoked among its tumblers of jam and cinnamon. The train, now that the doors had been closed again, was reasonably warm, as warm as it ever had been.

As I began my breakfast, I heard the shovels start work up the line. But no one else entered the dining-car. Presently the Spirit of Eating again rolled up to me. She posed a moment, looking with her stony, Cybele eyes. Then she said in her own odd French, "He would not wait. He got out and went on alone."

"Who, Madame?"

"Your friend."

"I haven't a friend in the world, Madame."

"The blond *monsew*," she said.

"Are you saying," I asked, "he left the train to walk?"

"Yes, *monsew*."

Oh, I was supposed to widen my eyes, and press her for more. How was this *possible*? Wasn't it *unwise*? Was he *insane*? I let her fill my cup with fur-black tea, and only said, "Then I expect he'll make the wolves wait their turn."

THE X'S ARE NOT KISSES

Tanith Lee and Esther Garber

After Jaidis had left, Emily decided to clean the flat, very thoroughly; what had once been called a Spring Clean. She began with the small bathroom, which was usually done once a week in any case, and went on to overhaul the kitchen area, scouring the stove, removing everything from the cupboards, washing and burnishing glasses. She went over the tiles with something supposedly miraculous she had seen in a TV advert, but the result was disappointing. Nevertheless, it produced a lovely smell.

Following this, Emily spent the weekend working on the large main room. She cleaned the long windows and the wide mirrors, shampooed the carpet, dusted down the curtains with an appliance on the hoover she had never used before. She polished the tables, and brushed the ornaments with a soft brush meant for a camera lens.

Outside the flat it was indeed spring, and Emily bought a dwarf laurel and two young bay trees.

Then, she stood outside the tiny bedroom that Jaidis had always used as her office and chamber of practice. Emily stood with her flaxen head on one side, wondering.

To clean or not to clean. This was the private room, which normally she had never entered, unless invited. Here Jaidis kept her accounts, typed her business letters, worked with her guitar, composed, or sometimes remained in profound silence, the door shut.

Emily retreated. She sat down on the couch in the main room, and thought about the thing she had thought about ever since Jaidis left. Which was, did Jaidis mean to come back?

There were three scenarios. First, that Jaidis would be gone for a week, ten days, a month, something like that. After which she would return and everything would resume as before. Secondly, that Jaidis would return, and explain to Emily that all was changed, and they must work something out, something that would be of course ultimately demoralizing and painful. The third possibility was that Jaidis would simply call her and say, "I'm sorry, Emily. But I'm not coming back. Can you pack up my things and send them on?"

It was really for this reason that, when Jaidis had specified that she would telephone Emily every evening, between six and eight, Emily had said, "Oh, no. You know how I sometimes have to work late. And any way, it will be difficult. Just phone me if you need anything." Jaidis had said at once, "You're determined to make this as bloody for me as you can, aren't you?" Emily did not say, *You are making things very bloody for me.* She did not even say, *Every time the phone goes, I shall feel sick with fear.* She said, "I'm sure, if it's as bad as it seems, you'll find it awkward to phone. Just – just call when you – when it's over." Which terrible double meaning only struck her later, once she was alone.

They had made love the night before Jaidis went away. Jaidis had been passionate and inventive, but Emily had had to pretend. Probably Jaidis knew this. But they did not discuss it, or anything. In the morning they had gone quickly through the budget for the month. Jaidis, a self-employed musician, tended to earn more but not on a regular basis.

Emily's job at the bookshop now provided the backbone for bills and rent. At ten, the taxi came, and Jaidis, with a fleeting kiss, went immediately towards the door, Jaidis dark as a shadow, graceful as a lion, and Emily stood there in her drained whiteness, with her heart exploding, dry eyed and smiling, not from pride, but from terror.

When the door shut, and she had heard the sound of Jaidis' light footfalls running down towards the street, the taxi starting, the wheels in the rain, Emily fell to her knees. After an hour pressed to the carpet, she saw the fluff that had got tangled into it with the tempest of her tears, and so decided on the spring cleaning.

They had met in the summer of the year before.

It was one of those rare, hot, perfect European nights that imply one might be anywhere short of the equator. Up on the terrace garden of the bookshop, there was a publicity party, with two quite well-known authors reading from their new books, bottles of cold wine, and an elegant buffet, complete with salmon and green seedless grapes.

Emily had wanted to work in the bookshop for some while, ever since she had gone past it every day, wretchedly on her way to somewhere not so nice. It was exquisitely clean, all glass and foot-deep plush, with escalators, a coffee-bar, and, best of all, stacks of books, the ancient and the modern, rising in tiers upon tiers, like a mountain built of words and dreams, life and fantasy. She had gone for her interview diffidently, but her instant mastery of the complex computer system, her knowledge of authors past, present and in embryo, and her undoubted, mostly unconscious, charm, saw her installed inside the week. She had been an employee only two months on the evening of the party. Emily had gone in a short black frock, with her blonde hair combed loose, not to entice, merely to be part of things.

The two authors were a fat woman with a mane of black and grey curls, and a thin old man in glasses with a slight stammer. Both read superlatively well, and afterwards came together over the wine. Here it was soon apparent that they had fallen in love. Quite literally that. For some reason they had never met before, and, as Emily discovered, they were both alone. Now their minds, bodies and spirits flew to meet, and a wonderful bloom of excitement rayed out from them, making them as heady to be near as two teenage lovers. Emily could have laughed aloud in pleasure. It was a marriage made in Heaven: her heavenly bookshop.

Half an hour later heaven provided some music, too.

There was a childlike quality to Emily, completely unirritating since she knew nothing about it. She went lightly through the crowd, and sat down on the clean paving, near enough to be able to watch the guitarist at her craft, what she did to draw the glorious alternating silver and contralto sounds from the instrument. At first Emily was only dazzled by Jaidis, who was, of course, entirely and defiantly dazzling. In innocence, Emily gazed on her, not thinking of herself at all.

Jaidis, Emily would have said, was a Negress – that title which, like Jewess, has had so many awful connotations, that, at one time it could not be employed without grave and unforgivable offense. However, Emily would internally have reasoned, the basis of the word had such intrinsic power – the two images of essence – *Black* (Negra) and *She* (the feminine ending), that for Emily it came at once. Guileless, clad in splendor, and empty of anything banal, let alone criminally insulting.

For Jaidis was like an empress. She was the Queen of Night.

Her blackness was deep as the sea. And from the blackness flowered the two black eyes that had in them, from the soft light of the terrace, hints of amontillado, even claret, and two crimson lips – the features of a fire god. Her hair was thick and woolen and grown long in plaits, through which sequins were woven. She wore a white dress, cut low, and over that a tight white waistcoat of silk, stitched with silver coins and stars.

Emily had been in love before, and already – the two authors – love was in the air. But oddly she did not recognize it. Even so, as she watched the hands of Jaidis on the opulent body of the golden guitar, her blood began to tingle. It made itself known to her that the black girl made love to the instrument, and *this* was how the music *came*. And so at last, even in the last chords, it occurred to Emily's flesh, if not to Emily, the question as to how it would be if she were the guitar, so plucked and stroked, so coaxed by those sliding fingers with nails of mother-of-pearl, so quietened, so tantalized, so brought to a final aching cry.

Emily got up. Her cheeks burned and she took a gulp of wine. And then Jaidis, smiling politely at the applause, glanced at her. Emily went forward, childishly, innocently. What might have been oppressive, even threatening in intent, was not, from her.

"That was so wonderful. I loved the Bach. And was it Rachmaninov? And the last one."

"The last one was mine."

"Oh," said Emily. It was as if she had seen her first Christmas tree, all bright with lights. And Jaidis it seemed had the wit to know that here was genuine praise, the true response the profound artist deserves and seldom receives, and then perhaps misunderstands, for it has come in the wrong dress.

But there Emily was, white as a feather in her black frock, and there black Jaidis in her white gown.

"May I get you some wine?" said Emily.

"Or I could share yours," said Jaidis.

Emily gave her the glass. As Jaidis' warm red lips touched the place where her own had been, the night blew up like a tent of fires, revealing all.

But though the two authors, he smiling and she laughing, got into the same taxi and were born away as if on wings, Jaidis and Emily parted at the door of heaven, with only a lunch date for the following day.

And after the lunch, at which Emily ate two mouthfuls of each course, and Jaidis rather more, and they had opened two bottles of Pinot Noir, they parted again, with only that dangerous flimsy thing between them, the number of a phone.

However, Jaidis rang Emily that night, just as the rosy sun was going down.

"Were you okay?"

"Oh yes. What do you mean?"

"We had rather a lot to drink."

Emily vaguely remembered floating about the bookshop all afternoon, particularly expert with the computer, almost to the point of the psychic. And then how a faint depression came, about five, and then the journey on the tube, and how the world had not seemed real, nor her room, and perhaps not herself, now.

Emily said she had been just fine.

Jaidis said, "I have to go up North tomorrow. A couple of bookings. I'm back next Saturday."

Emily tried to grasp the notion of the city, empty of Jaidis, therefore crumbling, falling, wrecked, until Saturday came.

Then Jaidis suggested that they have dinner tonight. And Emily said that was a very good idea, but it was her turn to pay for dinner, as Jaidis had paid for lunch, and Jaidis began to laugh.

"Why are you laughing?" asked Emily.

Jaidis stopped laughing. She said Emily's name. And when she said this, Emily knew that never in the world before had there ever been a woman called Emily.

The dinner was a foolish affair. They drank a little, but it was champagne, ate one course, or Jaidis ate it, and Emily inhaled it, toyed with it, left it in peace. A waiter arrived – it was a good restaurant – and asked if everything were quite all right.

"Quite all right," said Jaidis, "but we're in love."

The waiter grinned. He seemed pleased with them.

Never before had Emily heard anyone say anything so honest. And never again during the following months, did she hear Jaidis say anything of that kind or sort.

Not even when, curled in Jaidis' bed, among sheets like fires, Jaidis' skin upon hers, black, smooth, curiously sandy, caressing at every shift and breath, revealed the strawberry of her mouth, her inner mouth, rose in ebony, her hair that could slap and sting and tickle and slide, her strength, her sureness, the rasp of her cry, the beating of her live heart, not even then, not even after the song of Emily's orgasm, the stillness, the darkness, the dawn, not then, or after, the honesty: I love you. I am in love with you. My love. As if said once, never again need it be said at all. And Emily could honor this. It was almost unique. Like a comet. Once in a lifetime, yes, that should be enough.

In the morning, Jaidis went north.

A few weeks later they began to live together, Emily moving into Jaidis' flat. The area was better, and oddly it was easier to reach the bookshop from here. Jaidis had explained, she needed a little space of her own, a small physical space. To see to the boring bookwork of the self-employed. To practice, and to compose. From that room came the patter of the old typewriter, the marvelous convolutions of the guitar, a phrase hummed, curses, and affirmatives, silence.

Once or twice, Emily knocked, to offer coffee or tea, to inquire, in the first days, what Jaidis would like at the shops. These advances withered. Once in her chamber, the Queen of Night was isolate. True, it was only an hour or so, in the evening, a little more at weekends. And then too they would go walking, jointly shopping, to the cinema. And in the nights they would make love.

"I love you," Emily wished to say. It is natural to the child, the loving child. But she was cautious. A cautious child. A *well-mannered* child.

Of course, they talked a good deal of other things. Times, places, people – even, a little, of past affairs. Emily had been hurt now and then, and though she never complained, it seemed to her that Jaidis had not experienced hurt at all, had somehow avoided it, and did not refer to it ever because it was absent. This then gradually, as the days shortened, and the tube journeys became more neon and dull, formed an incoherent shape in Emily's mind, the shape perhaps of things to come. For if Jaidis had never been hurt, had she never loved enough to hurt, and therefore did she now? They were new lovers still. Fires flamed in them. And they were companionable. And Emily was all admiration – the beauty of Jaidis, her music, her independence – and Emily was so sweet, yes, so she had been told by others.

We are in love. She wanted to say to Jaidis in the black night that was her kingdom, "Do you love me still?" Like some girl in a tight bodice from an old romance. But Emily did not want to offend, or engineer. She did not want to force a lie, or worse, a painful truth.

Just before Christmas, Jaidis was away for four days, a lucrative assignment for the guitar. Emily, left alone, was a model of fortitude, although she could not sleep more than an hour or so each night, made mistakes on her friend the computer, broke a heel in the street, burnt out the kettle, and caught a cold.

Every night when Jaidis phoned her, Emily said nothing of all this, and was serene, loving and encouraging. She bought Jaidis an extra Christmas present, a long scarlet scarf shot with black and mauve. The evening when Emily came in and Jaidis was there, having caught an earlier train, some enormous tension seemed to let go of Emily's throat, and she burst out coughing for almost five minutes.

In the new year, Jaidis was away again, although only for two nights. Emily was much better at it now. She had even found some herbal stuff that helped her to sleep.

In February, a letter came.

Always, Jaidis would verbally dismiss her letters, some rude or importunate 'fan,' some tax demand. Now she said nothing, brooding over the single sheet of lined and tired-looking paper.

"Are you all right?" Emily said at length.

"Yes. It's this. I can't let you read it, it's very personal to her. A girl called Tina. Someone I used to know."

Emily for a moment felt as if far off, floating on a warm cloud of indifference, sorry only that Jaidis had been annoyed. And then the little needle came, that pierced her like a burning wire.

"Tina?"

"Tina. I haven't seen the woman for years."

Jaidis poured herself another coffee, and sat back, frowning. She had her lion's face, lean and fierce. She explained that Tina had been someone she had met, briefly. She did not say what had taken place between them, but perhaps, probably, this was obvious. Now Tina was in dreadful trouble, of some unspecified kind. Alone, distressed, reaching out.

"I'll send her fifty quid," said Jaidis. "It might help."

Although, up to a point, they pooled resources, their earned money was their own. Emily had no idea that the donation might be wrong. And yet, she did not like it, this sending of warm red notes to a secret woman called Tina.

But she said nothing; they did not discuss it further. Presumably the money went.

In the next week or so, Emily found herself looking out for an envelope in that disjointed yet sloping writing – the writing that had been on the envelope from the woman Tina, the envelope Emily had pulled out of the waste-bin. Nothing came. Nothing seemed changed.

February passed and was gone, and on the dark wet first Sunday of March, Emily and Jaidis walked over the common in their boots.

Emily stared about her. How bleak the trees before the buds, which were perhaps very late. And there a snow-drop crushed in the mud. There had been horrible frosts, and the early daffodils had died on the balcony.

"What's up?" said Jaidis.

"You could be lost here," said Emily, without thinking.

"No, I couldn't."

"Not you then. Someone. *I* could. Lost and never found."

"Let's walk over to the pub," said Jaidis. "You're cold."

In the pub they drank double whiskies and ginger, and there was a greyhound the color of a bullet, gentle as a dove. The mood changed.

Back in the flat waited muffins and butter, and lemons and cinnamon for the tea, but as they got in through the door, the telephone was ringing, and all at once, Emily stood aside. Jaidis answered the phone. She said, sharply, "*Tina—*"

Emily felt all the air go out of her, or was it her spirit? She became a flaccid skin dangling in the room.

She went to the bed behind the screen, sat down and pulled off her boots, and stayed still, listening.

"Yes," Jaidis said, over and over again. That was all. *Yes.* Finally the receiver was put down.

Emily came out and went to put on the kettle.

It was as she buttered the muffins that Jaidis came up into the kitchen and stood on the tiled floor and gazed at her.

"Look, Emily," said Jaidis, "I'm going to have to go off for a while. I don't mean an engagement to play. It's this girl, Tina. I have to, there isn't anyone else."

"Isn't there?" said Emily.

"No, I'm sorry. I can't break the confidence. It's foul. But I have to go. A week, a bit longer. Do you understand?"

Emily thought she did not, but how could she? Or did she only understand entirely? She wanted to say, *Don't go. I don't want you to go.* But that would be selfish and obtuse. She said, "No, of course."

Later, during the evening, they talked about how it would all be managed, and Jaidis said that, while away, she would phone, and Emily told her that it could be awkward, she had better not, and Jaidis became angry, which was perhaps some sliver of guilt over Emily piercing her armor.

That night, as Jaidis slept silently in their bed, Emily lay awake, as awake as when Jaidis had not been there. She thought, *I shan't sleep at all, once she goes.* But this did not seem so very awful, only like a tiny scratch when a sword had already gone through her vitals.

A few days after, Jaidis left. She took a cloth bag with her. She did not take the guitar. She wrote down a number where she might be reached, not, apparently the number of the woman Tina.

Emily had had a long talk with herself, a long continuing talk, through the sleepless nights, as Jaidis slumbered by her side, smelling of silk and sand, night and stars and blueberry soap, and – distance.

Emily had said, *You're being a fool. Tina is a friend. Jaidis wants to help her. This makes Jaidis just and kind.* But Emily said to Emily, *Your time is done. Tina is the true love. The real love. Everything is over now.*

Emily knew that others had left her before and not come back. But Jaidis was like no other.

To consider that Jaidis would really leave her for ever was un-thinkable. Emily could no more take it in than imagining that one day she would die. But one day she would, she would die. So why not this?

Outside the door of the hidden chamber, Jaidis' study or office or music-room, Emily stood again with the silly excuse of the dusting camera brush in her grip.

No, she did not want to tidy the room, that was not it at all. She wanted to go into it, as if she were going into Jaidis, not merely the obvious loving and sexual things – tongue, fingers – but her whole body entering Jaidis' skin or brain or soul. Emily was fully aware of this. She had already done the things that lovers did in novels – picked up an armful of sweaters from Jaidis' drawer and buried her face in them, gone to bed with Jaidis' summer jacket, in a vain attempt to sleep.

To go into the sanctum was somehow more finite.

She opened the door and entered, closed the door at her back, and was shut in.

Emily looked round. Of course, she had seen the room before, sat in it on the other chair when Jaidis had said, "Come and listen to this," playing over to her a fresh skein of music.

How empty now, this room. It was a hollow shell. And though a dim memory of Jaidis' perfume lingered, no real trace of her.

The guitar stood free, breathing, out of its case. The books on the shelves were in their usual orderly disarray. The typewriter had been covered against dust. Papers and leaflets, notepads and music paper and pens, littered the narrow table.

Emily sighed, for there was nothing for her here, and, against all common sense, she had thought there would be. She sighed, sighed, and half turned to go out again, and as she did, she looked straight at the little cabinet in the corner by the window. In there, she knew, were kept the adjuncts to the guitar, strings like strange hair, rubs and cloths to beautify it. And also, for once Emily had seen one placed there, certain letters that Jaidis wished to keep.

Emily had a dreary thought, a thought that was hurtful and drab together. She was acting like a girl from a book and was this because she had read so many books, and now could do no other? Could do no other than that which any heroine of any tale must now do.

She walked over to the cabinet and opened it – it had no lock. And there inside, was a pile of letters.

With a grimace – a genuine spasm of her facial muscles, which might have been distaste or anxiety or shame – or simply thoughtless fear – Emily drew out this pale heap and put it on the floor. She stood looking at it. The first and topmost letter was not that which had arrived from Tina. It was a friendly note from an arts centre in Birmingham, thanking Jaidis and asking if she would be free to come back in the summer next year.

Emily considered. After all, the cabinet had no lock. What could be concealed in it? But then, Jaidis would trust her. Emily had never – she had been so careful not to – pried.

The three scenarios ran swiftly through Emily's mind, like well-known playful rats. Jaidis would come back. Jaidis would come back and say, *Soon I will be gone for ever.* Jaidis would call and say, *I am already gone.*

Emily made a noise. It was repressed but hysterical. It mattered so much. Death was far away and could not be avoided, but this was life – this – this – *this.*

She knelt down and knocked the pile of papers apart, and found at their bottom a stack of typed manuscript, or so it seemed, held together by a large clip. At first she thought that Jaidis had written a short story, and felt a kind of wondering surprise, almost alarm, for it might not be very good, and had Jaidis hidden it for this reason, and after all she did not know Jaidis well enough – though they had been together for months – to guess if she might be a good writer or not – and anyway, what did this *matter?* And besides, it was not a story, for now she released the clip and turned the pages, she found the unmistakable ending of a letter, here, and then again, a friendly, loving letter, marked by something she herself had not used since childhood, in fact – two kisses written as X's, and beneath, sprawled bold and arrogant like ferns or flames, the penned signature *Jaidis.*

However, the top sheet did not begin like a letter. There was no introductory 'Dear.' There was no name. Oh, but it did begin, it did. It said, *My love.*

And next, below, it said, 'I loved you since I was a child. I loved you. How I loved you. And you never knew. Or did you know? But now I've looked into your eyes. Did you even see? I wanted to make you see. I'll make you see.'

Emily sat back. Almost without thinking, she beheld a date typed efficiently at the top of the page. It was about two years ago. Two years. And Jaidis had said, had she not, "I haven't seen the woman for years."

Although she then began to shake quite hard, Emily's brain seemed now to be crystal clear, and cool as ice.

She read the letter down. It was angry and impassioned. It hungered and did not expect to be filled. It ended, 'But I've lost you. Well, not quite. You're here in my body, in my music.' And then, two X's or kisses, and the signature.

Emily dropped the letter coldly and looked at the next. This was longer. And the date – the date was now only a few days after she and Jaidis had met – the time when Jaidis had first gone away. The greeting was more empowered. The words cascaded; in places run together:

'And I held you, your body inked in on the sheet, the flowers of your breasts and your vulva.'

Again, Emily paused. 'Inked in.' Tina was black then. Emily felt herself shrink and sere. She was colorless and scrawny. Opposites had not attracted. Like wished for like. How horrible she must seem, like a plant kept in the cellar and gone pallid, unsucculent.

And Jaidis had known Tina since childhood. Jaidis had given up, until, meeting her again—

'Again and again I made you catch on fire from me. You blossomed against me like a river that ran uphill. Your opened mouth, like a fruit, so sweet, and the roar of your heart in my ear. I could hear your heart even as I lay against your thigh. I could feel your heart inside my tongue, like a drum. And your heart resounded even before you cried aloud, as if your body knew before you did. And it did.'

"I shouldn't read anymore," said Emily. "This is private."

She thought, *There was no lock on the cabinet.* She had been meant to find it all. Ah yes. A *fourth* scenario. How easy it would be for Jaidis, when she telephoned. For then Emily would say, prim, anemic Emily, the wilted daffodil, "I know. Never come near me. I shall leave you. Good-bye." Or not, Good-bye – which meant God be with you. *No.*

She threw the letter away, far across the small room, and as it went, she saw three kisses on the end of the page, and the name

– or was it now only a *word*? – *Jaidis*. A word in a foreign language.

Emily stood up. She opened the door, leaving it open, and went to the kitchen and took a bottle of red wine, and opened that. She poured, not a wine glass, but one of the newly burnished Coke glasses, full. She drank as if very thirsty. And went back to the letters of her lover to another.

'You are dark as the night,' wrote Jaidis to her love. 'I never found such darkness. I get lost in the cloud of it. I smother in your flesh and I die. I want to die with your hands on my body, stretched out and howling. But I want to take you with me, and that's wrong. No, I want us to live. I want to make you come and build a cathedral out of your cries. I want to make a concerto of your cries. I want to curl up in your womb and you in mine. You're my child, I'm yours. I never loved anyone before. I wasn't alive. You frighten me, you're like a pillar, so smooth, impossible. Let me scale you. Let me pull you down.'

I want to cry, Emily thought, *but I can't.*

Nasty white scrawny tears.

How could she bear to touch me?

There were no longer dates, but the letters were many. They had met in the city, obviously, by day, when Emily worked in the heavenly bookshop, poor little idiot, earning the steady income that had made everything so much more monied and more safe.

But maybe Jaidis had tried to give Tina up. Yes, that must be so, because here, here:

'I hurt so much. I want so much from you. And I can't seize it. I daren't even ask. I must make do with what I've got.'

Make do. *She has made do – with me.*

Emily felt a surge of rage. She screamed aloud. She tore the letter in her hands, across, across. And its wicked kisses, she broke them.

Tina had given Jaidis the letters back, evidently. And Jaidis had put them away. But neither had been able to bear it, that making do. At last Tina wrote to Jaidis – not a typed, orderly letter, but that sodden little scrap – how clever, how irresistibly vulnerable. Had fifty pounds gone to Tina as a result – or more likely another of those fires, this currency of the loins and heart. And so at last, the telephone. And Jaidis, with her face so weary, as perhaps she might one day look when she was very old, as now Emily would never see. "I'm going to have to go away for a while."

She had left everything. Even she had left the golden guitar. Jaidis did not care. *Love moves the sun and the other stars.*

Emily got up. She had been impertinent enough to enter Bluebeard's chamber, and found the secret, and now she would die.

Emily stared myopically. Her Coke glass was empty. She must get more wine. Her life was empty. Another letter had fluttered up in her hand. She glanced at it.

'I will die of you. I could shake you. Like the magic tree, would you then let loose your fruits? I will have the curve of your stomach, the angle of your knee, the turn of your head, the chains of your hair, the soft gates of your mouths. But what else can I do with you? You strike me dumb. Damn you. No, I want only the best for you. I wish I could eat you, from the soles of your feet to the crown of your head. But I only want to sit at your feet and sing.'

Four kisses. There were four.

How curious, this affectionate token, the plaything of the casual pen. X's for kisses, after such an outcry.

But now she was gone. She was with Tina. No more need for letters. Kisses to be implanted like burning spears.

Emily let go the letter, let go of Jaidis, and let go of her own self with them.

For a few days more, Emily marked time, as sometimes after a great shock it is necessary to do, even with rescue in sight.

Then she went one evening to the local surgery, at which she had registered all those months before.

She knew what to say, for modern novels were full of it. There was a lot of stress at work, and she simply could not sleep. She understood she could be given a few sleeping pills, perhaps enough for ten days, just to break the pattern of her insomnia. She did not want to resort to them really, but she did need to sleep, or she could not cope.

The doctor was sympathetic, demonstrably liking her general health, intelligence, and her resistance to the possible risk of addiction. He gave her twenty-eight tablets, told her to take them for two weeks now, and keep the rest for future use, if necessary. He warned her that these pills were strong, and she should drink absolutely no alcohol while taking them. Emily promised that she would not, thanked him and left. She was very relieved, because twenty-eight pills, together with a bottle of wine, seemed certain to do what she wished. She had been afraid she would have to top up the medication with antihistamines, or codeine, not sure of the result.

The dusk was early, and Emily went through it like a shadow, back to the flat. She had not said good-bye to the bookshop. Why should she think it had liked her? She checked carefully in the flat, as at the shop, that she had left everything pristine and in order, the slight washing-up dried and put away, a stack of clean towels in the cupboard. Her own belongings she had placed in two cardboard boxes from the grocers. There was no relative or friend who would want anything, need anything, but the items might bring pleasure somewhere. Emily had not bothered to make a will, but then she had no savings of any importance. She felt Jaidis any way would not want her money, it might seem callous or recriminating to leave it to her. The contents of Emily's wallet, two twenty-pound notes and a ten, she left on the coffee table. The eight loose pound coins she would need, for the wine and her traveling expenses.

Of course, Jaidis would now have to come back to the flat, but that again might be an advantage. Jaidis might like to keep the flat for herself and Tina. She might in any case have had to ask Emily to vacate the premises, and that would have been awful for both of them.

When Emily had finished, she drew the curtains back to let in daylight tomorrow for the plants. Outside, the laurel, full of rain, seemed bright as a jewel with new spring growth. Jaidis would like the laurel and the bay trees. It was good to have left something lovely behind, in return for the lovely times. For the agony there could be no return. It was too vast. And she could not hurt Jaidis. Jaidis was immune to her.

Outside there was only a faint drizzle now, and all the lights of the world seemed rolling and flashing through and into it. It appeared a cheerful evening, everyone going home to their hearths or else rushing out to places of enjoyment. Emily looked about her sadly. She wished none of them any ill.

The off-license was full of choice wine, and she bought a bottle of dark red, which the man assured her, although she had not asked, was a real winner for £5.92. She put it in her bag, which also contained the sleeping pills, and the corkscrew she had bought yesterday. She had not wanted to take the corkscrew from the flat.

Emily caught a bus, a red wet bus all lit with lights, and let it carry her up through the neons and the dark and the rain, towards the common.

People were talking and laughing on the bus, shaking themselves like wet dogs. There seemed a general mood of optimism and camaraderie. Even the driver, taking her fare, smiled at her, and Emily had smiled back.

She thought how strange it was she felt no anger now, and very little pain. She did not feel desperate or tragic or even crucial. All that had passed. This must be because she knew she would not have to suffer. Although once, it suddenly occurred to her, as if she had not realized until then, *I am going to kill myself tonight.* And she experienced a sort of startlement, as if she had just looked down and seen that she was floating several inches in the air. Even so, even though it must be unreal, and curious, she knew it would happen. She did not want to change her mind. She never even thought to herself how much she had loved Jaidis, to be driven out to do this. She did not see herself anymore doing anything, really. She was no longer the heroine of her own story, who must be evaluated, psychoanalyzed. The heroine had ceased to exist.

When they reached the edge of the common, Emily got out, and the bus hissed away from her and its radiance was gone. She walked up into the woods.

She took the path she had always taken with Jaidis, from force of habit, and since, in the dark it was difficult to find a way, for the lights here were few and far between.

So she came, after about half an hour, to the spot where she had said before that she could be lost. She recognized it, even in the dark, and, perhaps, had recognized it formerly, its possibilities. There was a steep dip where the trees clung close, and so a chance that if she went down into this part, no one would find her, or if they did, not for some while. She did not want to be found at all. She did not want to upset anyone. It was not their fault.

She got into the dip easily, sliding a little on the mud and last year's leaves, and so pushed through into the middle of the trees. Here she sat down.

She felt like a child now. But it was not the charmingly unconscious childishness others perceived; this was a feral child, lost in the forest. She had not left a trail of beans or rice to follow home.

Emily took out the bottle of winning wine and opened it with the corkscrew. She drank two mouthfuls, and all at once was apprehensive. She did not want the wine, and must consume the whole bottle. She should have brought water—

But then, she could not have been sure.

She would wait a minute. Wait for the first mouthfuls to relax her.

Above, through the rain-dropped boughs of the trees, she could see the drops of the stars. And on the branches too were visible other abrupt points, the spring buds finally breaking. Below, buses and cars rumbled. A plane threaded the night. She felt very calm. She drank another sip of wine – save plenty for the pills. Yes, it was better now. How nice the wine was after all. But she must get on. She had been here a long while, perhaps an hour. It seemed to have been an hour, or even more, time contracting, passing through another dimension, as sometimes it had done during the insomnia, the spaces between one and six a.m. lasting a month, or vanishing in a few minutes.

Emily put her hand into the bag and touched the sleeping pills in their neat flat box – and in that instant, heard someone coming up the path, up from the road so far below.

There was no need to worry about this. Emily must only stay still. The nocturnal traveler would go by.

But the footsteps, a woman's it seemed, came striding, swift and harsh, over the debris of the path, right up to the dip. And then, as it might have done in a nightmare, a torch flashed down, straight into Emily's eyes, into her body, like a knife.

"Emily!" shouted a hard and brutish and terrible voice. "*Emily!*" And Emily cowered, no longer feral, no longer calm, frightened to the brink of madness. She dropped the bottle in this state, and heard it splash away its vital, needful fluid, and a tiny noise escaped her.

Then the beast from above, with its eye of torch, came crashing down into the dip tearing through the boughs of trees, kicking at the shale, growling and snarling.

Emily jumped to her feet, but she could not run away, there was no room to do so. And now the beast, burning and roaring, took hold of her.

The torch was clamped between them, and by its glare, Emily saw upward now into the lion face of night, which had formed itself into this shape, and come to engulf her: Jaidis, Jaidis furnace hot and smelling of feverish skin and perfume and the smoky taint of trains.

"What are you doing here?" said Jaidis, almost in her normal voice, just a little hoarse, breathless.

"That's my question," said Emily, remotely. Of all unreality this was the most unreal. This could not be, and was not. Had she already taken the pills, and was she now hallucinating? Well, she could talk to the hallucination of Jaidis. It was nice, really, she had not thought they would meet again. Be grateful then, Emily. "You look tired," said Emily, "Jaidis."

Jaidis swung her a little, pushed her a little away, yet kept firm hold of her.

"What I'm doing here, is finding you," said Jaidis. "I saw you as you came out of the flat. I was across the road. I called to you but you didn't hear. So then I followed you. "

"I didn't see you," said Emily. She was sleepy, and wanted to lay her head against Jaidis' breast. But obviously Jaidis was not really there.

"No, I don't think you did. I stood outside the off-license," said Jaidis, "and I waited for you to come out. Something was keeping me back, you see. You looked so bloody strange. I didn't want to scare you. And then I meant to speak to you as you came out again, with that bottle of wine. I thought, somehow she knows I've come back, and the wine's to celebrate. Yes, that'd be good. But your face."

Emily smiled. She did not know why.

Jaidis said, "And when you came out, you looked straight through me. Do you know that? Straight through me, Emily, and you walked on, and then you caught a bus."

"Yes, I did," said Emily. She amended, "But I didn't see you."

"I know you didn't. You bloody didn't. Christ, Emily. It was like— No it was worse. It was much worse."

Emily said, "I read your letters, you see."

"What letters?"

"The letters you wrote to – Tina."

"How could you read it," said Jaidis, "there was only one, I sent that. You mean you read it before I sent it?"

"The letters in your cabinet," said Emily softly. "I'm sorry, I know I shouldn't have. The letters that had kisses at the end."

"Kisses..." said Jaidis.

There was a silence.

Emily said, "Were you on the bus?"

"The bus," said Jaidis, "no, I just stood there. And then I got a taxi."

"To follow the bus," said Emily.

"The bus was gone. I knew you were coming here."

"Yes," said Emily.

Jaidis let her go. Jaidis said, "When I first met you, you didn't see me. And you didn't tonight."

Emily said, "I want to sleep now. Thank you for being with me. I did love you."

"You mean you loved me and now you don't love me?"

"Oh yes," said Emily, "always. And I hope you'll be happy with Tina."

"For God's sake," said Jaidis, "I went to see Tina because her husband left her. I can't go into details, it isn't my secret. But she's okay now. She's with a man now, a man she likes. All right?"

"You loved her," said Emily, "since childhood."

"She wasn't even a friend," said Jaidis with a terribly cold scorn. "But I owed her a favor. A big favor. I've paid it back now."

"But the letters were to Tina," said Emily.

"*Those* letters," said Jaidis. She drew in her breath. She put back her head, and Emily stared in wonder at the ebony column of her throat, pulsing with life. "No, not Tina."

Emily laughed. Her legs gave way gently and she dropped through Jaidis' aura and sat on the muddy earth. It was so interesting, this. It was so mild. And soon she would sleep, and then she would die, going out with this memory.

"Listen to me," said Jaidis, now beside her, shaking her, Jaidis no longer burning with heat, but only warm, physically present, positive. "What have you done? Have you taken something?"

"Yes. Something nice."

"*What?*"

"All the sleeping pills. I don't remember, but I have, and the special wine."

"The wine's spilled," said Jaidis. Her voice was like a sword. "Give me your bag." And Emily let Jaidis take the bag, and out of it Jaidis presently produced the packet of sleeping pills, intact, unopened. "These? The seal isn't broken."

"It must be," said Emily. She was not alarmed.

"Was there anything else?"

"No. They should be enough, shouldn't they?"

"Maybe not. But you haven't had them."

"Oh," said Emily. Her brain began to rinse itself like a plate under a tap. Everything was sluicing off, and here she was, wide awake, cold, sitting next to Jaidis under the trees. And Jaidis was real. "I've done everything all wrong," said Emily.

"Get up," said Jaidis. They rose. "We'll go back to the flat," said Jaidis.

"No," said Emily. "I can't. Not now. Not after the letters."

"*Shut up*," Jaidis screamed at her. In amazement Emily turned to see. Jaidis' face was full of a fearsome savagery. Her eyes were wide. She looked capable of killing Emily on the spot. Far away, a dog barked; it had heard the roar of the lion in the wood. "Those letters," Jaidis said. She lowered her voice like a weapon. "Those letters were to you."

"To me?" Emily asked politely.

She was not going to die. She was not dreaming this. It was not mildness but uncouth lies.

Nevertheless Jaidis looked as if she had been badly hurt, mauled perhaps by her own persona, turning.

Emily said, "I've made an awful mess of this. I'm sorry. I'll just go down. It's all right."

"Emily, *listen*. The letters were to you. Things I couldn't say. So I wrote to you. It started years ago."

"How can it have?" asked Emily. She felt numb and temporarily quiet, between onslaughts, as if after some successful minor surgery of which the outcome remained unsure.

"What do you mean," said Jaidis in turn, "*how?*"

"I remember the letters," said Emily. "You met her two years ago."

"I met *you* two years ago," said Jaidis, her eyes flat as inverted stars. "I met you in a restaurant, and you waited on my table. I tried to find a way to talk to you, but the place was full and I was with two other stupid people. When I went back, you'd left."

Emily, surprised, said, "Yes, I was a waitress. And you—"

"You didn't even see me," said Jaidis. "And then you'd gone. I wrote you the first letter then. I wrote you three songs, too. I thought you were gone for good."

"I did a lot of horrible jobs," said Emily, vaguely. "I never stayed anywhere for long. But – how can I not have seen you?"

"You didn't. Have you ever?" Jaidis said.

"You're all I see," said Emily. She lowered her eyes. Perhaps it did not matter if she told the truth at last. For what Jaidis spoke could not be the truth at all.

"You don't see me," said Jaidis. "You see skin and hair and eyes and bones." She struck herself in the upper stomach, hard, a blow. "I'm *here*."

Emily flinched, frowned. "I know. I see that you, too. "

"I wrote you the letters because I didn't dare say those things to you," said Jaidis. "I didn't know what you'd do. So quiet and controlled and well-mannered and gentle. I could make you come. That was good. That was the only time the guard went down. But did you pretend? No, not with that heartbeat. That was *real*. So I wrote about that."

"You said you loved me – her – since you were a child," said Emily. She was abruptly defiant. She raised her head and stared into Jaidis' face. "Even if I did meet you two years ago, how can I have known you as a child?"

"I didn't say you did," said Jaidis. "I knew *you*. I had a fantasy friend when I was little. I loved her. I told my sister and got a lot of shit because my secret friend was white and had blonde hair. I learned to shut my mouth. When I was about fifteen, I started looking for her, Emily, looking for you. And once or twice I thought I found her. But I hadn't. And then, I did. I did, Emily. Once, and you were gone. But then, that second time."

"At the shop," said Emily. She considered how Jaidis looked at her, and they had shared the wine. It was not like a first meeting. It was as if prearranged. Fate.

"The second letter," said Emily, harshly now, also lifting her voice up to meet the voice of Jaidis, so cruel and iron under the trees: Duelists. "That love letter—"

"To you, when I went away. After our first time. Another typewriter I borrowed for some business letters. The spacebar kept jamming."

Emily said, "The words ran together."

"That's why."

Emily raised her fists now. She cried out. "You wrote she was inked in – *inked* in – she's black, she's black, Jaidis. You wrote it—"

Jaidis said, her voice falling back now through the air, "A line-drawing. Your whiteness on the darkness of the sheet. You seemed to have a line drawn round you."

"Dark as night," said Emily, "*that's* what you said."

"You are," said Jaidis. "I don't mean *skin*. I mean the bloody cloud in you. The dark cloud that I can't get by."

"But I love you," said Emily. "And you never said that you loved me."

"Neither did you," said Jaidis.

"Why did you never *tell* me—"

"Why didn't you?"

Emily stepped back. She drew down her hands and folded them, like a good child. "When I saw you at the shop, when you played your guitar, I thought you were the queen of night. I'm sorry that I love your blackness, I don't mean to be insulting. I never even had a real friend who was black. But when I saw you, you were like – a black torch, a black *fire*. All right, it's the outer casing and you're inside. But I love both. The look and smell and taste of you, your eyes like that sky up there, but with *red* stars, Mars stars – and your hair that's so soft and so – so almost sticky – and *alive* – and the paler lovely line behind your ears, and the pink flush behind your knees, and your nails and your palms like the inside of a rose – a *black* rose – and in your vagina, there, flames in a coal – and how white your teeth are, and your eyelashes, and how your spine looks like a snake under your skin. And I love your music that you play in your room when I creep up and lean on the door to listen so I won't disturb you. And the way you listen to a book when you read it – yes, I can see you *listening* to the words – and the way you breathe when you sleep, and the thoughts behind your eyes. And all of you inside I love, all I know. But I've never known very much, you've never told me. And I want to be told. I wish I'd been there when you were a child, I'd have made them like me, even your sister, or I'd have made them put up with me. And we would have been together all the time we could. I never had a proper friend. I wish it had been you. I want to be with you now. I want to be with you when I'm old and you're old, some cranky old lady, thin and stooping and graceful and bony, and your hair grey. And if there's anything when we die, I want to be with you then. For as long as there is. And for ever if there is for ever. And if not, for now. At least, that. Please." Emily undid her hands. She said, "Please."

Jaidis stood before her and was silent.

Then at last she said, "Of course we'll live forever. You only really want what you can have."

They went down the hill not touching, and when they were at the bus stop, they began to brush the mud off each other, and made it worse. It looked as if they had been coupling in the wood, rolling and biting and shrieking in a sexual frenzy. By the time the bus came they were laughing so much that the driver grinned. Two pretty girls come from some office party. Well, live and let live.

In the dark, Emily sentimentally murmured, "And the dear kisses on the letters."

"Not kisses," said Jaidis. "The X's aren't kisses. They were the times I came. Alone, the first time, thinking of you. And then the times *with* you."

"Like the marks on an airplane," said Emily. "Shot down."

"Little deaths," said Jaidis.

"Five tomorrow," said Emily, "if you write to me."

To herself, as Jaidis slept, Emily mused dreamily on and on, and round and round, easing towards sleep as if across a smooth deep pool.

Emily thought, *The X's are not kisses. They are the unmarked and uncharted lands on a map, the map of the heart. Yes, that's it. And in those lands we must always speak the heart's truth, to be understood. Whatever the cost. And if you speak this truth and someone strikes you in the face for it, you must turn to the next one the other cheek. Yes, you must, over and over. For one day it may not be a blow, but a kiss.*

Judas Garbah

My mother gave parties. Or, they were soirées. Cheap, shoddy soirées – and only gentlemen attended, though her maid served the drinks.

I was three or maybe just four. The maid bathed me angrily and washed my hair, getting soap in my eyes, and hurting me. I was a nuisance. Sometimes, though, she was gentle in her way, Chushi – the name I called her, probably remembered wrongly. When gentle, Chushi would smother me to her bosom, cradle me, saying that I was a poor child, a poor neglected child. My mother, in moments of what she herself called 'Tenderness,' did something similar, but she touched less. She would put me back and stare at me, murmuring, "So pretty. What a pretty little boy." So the poor child, the pretty little boy, learned early, as do we all, his nature and his names.

We'd lived before in a crumbling tenement, and been saved from it to live in this other crumbling tenement, whose greenish walls decayed down into a river, which – presumably – was the Nile, or some off-shoot of it. I had played in the mud sometimes with Arab children who found me unwholesome, too pale, and slow to learn. They'd jeer at, beat or trick me. Now and then they drove me off completely and I lurked at corners, watching them. Their dirty vibrant solid world looked good to me. But I was already better fed, and I stank of being occasionally bathed. Mariamme, my mother, always tried to stop me playing with Arab boys; Chushi therefore did the same. But mostly they didn't like me in the way. I spent a lot of time in my own room, which was narrow and damp. A tutor came at irregular intervals. Rather than teach me anything, he told me stories of his life. But I had no complaints. Everything different was of interest to me.

Tonight's party, or soirée, for which I was being bathed, was apparently important. I was taken out of my room for important ones. I would make a brief appearance, or longer, if the guests showed approval. But my character often changed. I wasn't always Mariamme's son, but sometimes the son of her sister, or an orphan boy she'd seen and bought, with French banknotes, from his destitute parents.

Mariamme came into my room at sunset, when the mystic Cry was going up from the prayer towers.

She wore a beaded coppery dress over her satiny amber skin. Mariamme had a tendency to fat. She would eat nothing but sweetmeats if left to herself, and she liked cocktails, too. At other times she starved, taking only water. The general effect was voluptuous, very attractive and honeyed, for certain men. She had a hooked nose, black eyes, black hair thickly curled. A salamander, yes that fits.

"How lovely," she said, looking at me. "Judas, you're a little doll of a boy. Yes, you are. Made all of *loukoum*." Then, frowning, "What's that on his cheek?"

"A scratch," said Chushi.

"Powder over it. Powder his face. You careless boy!"

"He fell," said Chushi laconically. Actually, she had caught my cheek with the comb. She was always rough, even in her gentle hugs and rockings, which made one seasick.

"Never mind," said Mariamme. Dismissing not the scratch but my discomfort.

She stood looking at the rubber-red sun sinking behind moody water, dim domes, and cut-paper-fronded palm trees. (This marvelous view, for which a tourist might have committed murder, we rarely appreciated.) She gulped her current cocktail down, and burped, an indulgence allowed only before us.

"Your dress is creased," she said to Chushi. "Didn't you iron it?"

"Oh, yes," lied Chushi, who only ironed her hair.

There were three gentlemen that night. They sat in a half circle, round Mariamme's divan. I sat on a stool to one side fencing uneasily with a monkey one of the men had brought with him, his pet. It kept trying to bite me – Oh, familiar scenario. Everyone hated little Judas. I was frightened of the monkey, though the man had put us together at once. As if being both small, that should make us friends. He had also added slyly, "Watch he doesn't bite you. Only me he never bites."

Chushi clucked disapprovingly at the monkey. She equated all animals as vermin, rats, cats, monkeys. Only animals that could be eaten were worth anything. She'd often praised to me a goat of her father's that was so very intelligent, and had tasted delicious.

The cocktails were sweet, reminiscent of kerosene. Sometimes Mariamme made me taste one, or she gave me as a treat the cherry from her drink. When I was two she slapped me before her guests for gagging and crying at the burn of the alcohol. Someone quipped I had been born an abstainer. Was it after that party Mariamme tried to lose me in the city? (Maybe not. Anyway, it happened many times.) She would drink heavily; and next day a madness of depression set in. She would then lead me out, her eyes leaden, looking like what at first she must have been, an inexpensive whore of the alleys. In the midst of a busy street she told me to wait, by a Jewish shop. Then she went away. An hour later, the old Jew came out and found me there. You expect now I'll tell you he was kind, gave me a cup of milk, and bore me home, to my unwilling mother. But oh no. He drove me off, lashing with his arms, cursing me in Hebrew. I then spent some hours roaming about. I think I cried, but can't remember. I should have been swept away, grabbed for some brothel or simply killed in passing by someone or other. Instead, by peculiar accident, I finally saw Chushi, creeping back to the flat from some villainy, and running up, grasped hold of her skirt. "You!" she exclaimed. "She won't like you being *here*." And home we went. Mariamme, when she woke from her drugged sleep, seemed to have forgotten everything. But afterwards, like the children in fairy tales, I memorized landmarks on every outing, and now and then found I'd needed to. Twice she left me in the same café. I stayed until midnight, when I was put out, both times to clear the place for a band of robbers. The apartment doors were locked when I got back, and no one would let me in until dawn, when the sweeper came.

It was a sort of amnesia with Mariamme. She forgot me, and then forgot she had forgotten me.

One of her men asked her one day (night), why she gave me this doomed, Christian name. She shrugged. She had some ridiculous reason. But really she had forgotten who Judas was supposed to be.

In the end, the monkey noticed something moving behind the cabinet, no doubt a rat, the large black kind from the building. The monkey stole away, and I was able to relax a little. It was then I saw one of that night's beaux was watching me.

When he saw me looking, he smiled, but I didn't smile back. I knew no one was to be trusted, that I was pretty, neglected, and quite unlikable. If they hated me, and tried to pretend the opposite in order to trick me, why help them? Presently he put the smile out and glanced away.

Soon after this my mother asked me to recite a poem the tutor had, in a moment of aberration, taught me.

I saw all the faces in the room but hers set in a ghastly rigor: The reciting child.

Quickly I shuffled the verses in my head, selected one that was short, and said it clearly, putting in the commas, as my tutor had expressed it.

"*Alexandre te veut...*"

It took one minute. I was applauded, obviously for being so quick. Mariamme looked disappointed. "No, no, there was more, about the horse – you've left it out—" "He did very well, Madame," said the man who had smiled at me. "But I too know this poem. *Boucephalon, with his eyes of blackest flame – the Ox-Star on his brow – that Alexander loved more than his lovers, who – never bore him with that pride – not truly knowing him to be a god.*"

"And the boy's been taught *that*?" asked the fat man with the monkey. "No wonder he left it out."

From behind the cabinet came screeches. The monkey had met the rat and probably they had both bitten each other.

Everyone jumped up, my mother screaming, the fat man in great fear for his pet.

I found myself left behind with the man who had smiled.

As the others scrabbled at the cabinet, hefting it so things inside fell over with a crash, coaxing and shouting, he said quietly to me, "Do you understand the poem?"

Under all circumstances, I must be polite. But I need not smile. I said, "Alexander loved him, but only the horse loved Alexander as he should be loved."

"Loved whom?" asked the man, who was old and straight and smelled clean and fragrant. By which I mean he seemed all that. And he was probably about twenty-six. The fat man had brought him with the monkey.

"Loved—" I stumbled on the Greek name, "Lukestion."

"Does that seem strange to you?" asked the old young man.

I was silent. No. It didn't seem strange. I hadn't thought about it.

"For a man," he said, "to love another man – in that way."

"What way?" Who cared?

He said, "I'll teach you two new words. A woman who loves another woman is called for an island, Lesbos, a Lesbian. But a man who loves another man is called for Alexander, who was the son of a god, and loved men, and for his city by the sea, Alexandria. An Alexandrian." He touched my head softly. His hand was cool in the hot, cocktail-fumey night, and he cool and calm, keeping us beyond the noise and upheaval, the monkey-business at the cabinet. "Will you be an Alexandrian, Judas?"

I glanced up at him then. His face was intent, actually innocent. Do I mean naïve.

"I'd like," he said, "to take you to a courtyard that has a beautiful green cistern, and lamps that shine in the water. But you're much too young, and he'd kill me. He likes women, too, you see. But *we* must all be faithful. Can you imagine it for me, one night, Judas, sitting by the green pool with me? *Je te veux...* By the time you're ready, I'll be old. It took me by surprise. I didn't know one could fall in love at sight, and with a child. Will you tell her this, what I've said, your mother? Please don't. I don't trust your mother. She might bring you to me— Don't. Whatever you do, don't tell her."

From his hand resting on my hair a wave of tingling newness poured all through me. I wanted to fall down asleep or otherwise unconscious at his feet. Have him pick me up, myself boneless. Take me to the courtyard with the pool. There we would be, and do what? Flickerings moved in my belly. Something stirred, a snake. Then I felt very sick, and ran quickly out of the room, to the place with the bucket, where I threw up violently. Chushi would curse me when she found it, my sick in her bucket. One more mess.

No one – but for him, presumably – noticed I didn't come back. The monkey was extricated and taken at once away. Glasses had been smashed. The party also broke up in confusion, and my mother drank herself into stupor, and, late the next day, took me out to lose me somewhere.

It was Chushi who found me in the bazaar, with the lights strung up on wires, and naphtha torches. She'd been looking for me. It was I who'd dawdled.

Although I never saw him again, for years I would lie in bed, and think of the cistern and the man's hand on me, riven with glorious swirling excitements, tingles and surges that seemed to have no beginning and could bring no end, but which at last drew the snake upright on its rosy stem. I must have been seven by then, and reaching out to hold the snake, knew in stages that he too took me somewhere, and went with him, and arrived, and was lost.

But you still come back, that's the problem with it.

DEATH AND THE MAIDEN

Esther Garber

ONE

St John Blaze was famous as a skilled, romantic painter, somewhat affiliated to the Pre-Raphaelite school – and also for many rumored exploits. One of these being that he tended to mix up his more complex colors on the back – and backside – of the latest nude model, using her as a palette.

Ruth met Blaze's wife by chance at a charity event in London.

"Oh! There's Lady Vera Blaze."

"Vera?" asked Ruth.

"It's a Russian name. She has Russian blood, I believe. Isn't that superb? And so suitable, as she's married to St John Blaze."

Ruth had been press-ganged into assisting at a stall that sold beads and ribbons. She wondered how this had happened – some stillborn promise to a friend who hadn't understood how to take *yes* as the true answer of *no*. After the first twenty minutes of playing with the colors of the ribbons, Ruth had grown leaden and bored. She was also growing into the floor of the large room with its fake palms and slow-moving crowds, dying of yawning.

But now here was Melisande Crabtree, chattering as usual in her cage-bird way. (*Melisande.* Anything less like…poor thing, with her long red nose and frantic crooked hat. But these archaic names were all the fashion now. Lord Tennyson's poetry, and the sumptuous work of the Pre-Raphaelites, had seen to that.)

"Look!" cried Melisande, her nose blushing more deeply, "she's coming this way."

Ruth raised her heavy head and boredom and ennui fell from her with a resounding crash.

Vera Blaze was a tall, broad-shouldered, elegant woman. She wore a costume of midnight blue, simple as only wealth allowed. Her dark hair, piled up in coils under her wide hat, framed a strong face of high Slavic cheekbones and slanting golden cat-like eyes.

She moved in on their stall with the striding walk of a woman more used to horse-riding and, you suspected, trousers, in the freedom of her own home.

"Oh, good morning, Lady Vera," stammeringly twittered Melisande.

"Hello, Melly. How are you? Good," said Vera Blaze, dismissing Melisande with absolute politeness.

Look at me, thought Ruth. *No, you won't.*

New-made aristocrats were always the worst, and after all Blaze had only been knighted last year.

Vera leaned forward a little and ran some of the ribbons through her fingers, dismissed them also, picked up a long strand of sea-green beads.

"Remind me," she said, to Melisande, "what this is all about."

"The charity we're supporting? Oh, it's Northern Orphans, Lady Vera."

"Indeed. Is it? Are there many?"

"Oh, yes, Lady Vera. The mining disaster at—"

"Yes. I remember. You'll think me callous," she added, turning abruptly her amazing tiger's eyes full blast on Ruth, who felt herself inwardly sway at the impact, "but I attend such quantities of these things." She held out her hand, immaculately gloved, and Ruth shook it. Even the glove was electric, of course. "Blaze," said the tiger. "Vera. And you?"

"Ruth Isles."

"Miss Isles, I believe I'll take some of these beads. My daughter will like them. At least, I hope so."

"You have a daughter, Lady Vera?" Ruth asked, bemused. For how could this creature reproduce anything but lynxes?

"Yes. A young girl. About your age, I suppose. But then not so young that it means *I* am young anymore."

"Oh, Lady Vera!" cried poor Melisande flirtatiously, but excluded to the outer reaches of the stall that were now about a hundred miles away.

Ruth said, "I'm not so young either, Lady Vera."

"Do drop the *lady*. It's tiresome. *He* dislikes it too," she added with an unmistakable, offhand contempt. "He wanted it so much, that rap on the shoulder by a sword – but *Sir St John* sounds quite stupid, don't you think." Melisande bubbled with shock. Ruth grinned. "Melly," said Vera, turning back to her, gracious and certain, a fine commander giving perfectly reasonable orders, "you take over this stall, will you?"

"Oh – but Lady Ver—"

"Parcel up all those beads for me, there's a dear. Here. A pair of guineas."

"But Lady Ver – that's far too mu—"

"For those orphans of yours. And I'll just borrow Miss Isles a moment. I really must have someone show me where the tearoom is."

Ruth found herself plucked instantly away, swimming strongly through the currents of meandering ladies, side by side with Vera Blaze. Melisande was left behind, an astounded shipwreck among the guineas and the beads.

They drank tea at a table under a tall window, with a view of the self-absorbed city rushing by below, carriages, horses, and people.

"Northern Orphans," mused Vera Blaze. "That, if abbreviated to its first letters, unfortunately spells *NO*. Not an augur, I trust." She had removed her gloves to reveal wonderful practical hands, scarred across the fingers and palms by either hard gardening or horse-pursuits – or both. Ruth noted the golden wedding-ring, broad, and engraved by some classical design. Also a tawny polished stone worn on the right hand.

They had not talked about art. Ruth, who had no interest at all in St John Blaze, or his paintings, had sensed she was not now alone in that. Vera's conversation concerned the state of London architecture, politics – briefly – and a 'ludicrous' soirée she had been to the night before. She made Ruth laugh at every juncture. Vera's awareness of the absurd seemed finely tuned.

Then: "How I long to get home," she announced. "London is always itself. But the countryside, even my countryside so close to the city, is never the same two days running. Also I can smoke at home after my cup of tea. I have a brand of cigars made especially for me in the South Americas. Delicious. I wonder if you'd like them."

Ruth said, "If you did, I'm sure I should."

"What an obedient girl you are."

"I only follow those worth following," said Ruth, recklessly perhaps.

But Vera Blaze merely said, "One prays your judgment, then, is never faulty."

"Often," said Ruth. "But sometimes true excellence is so overwhelming, even *I* can't miss it."

Vera turned and again looked straight into Ruth's eyes, dazzling her. "The young go so fast," she said.

"Like a runaway train," said Ruth, her self-control changing to butter; malleable, salty, tasty.

"Well," said Vera, "perhaps I should take you home with me." Ruth's heart bounded to a stop and fell over, panting, on the floor of her ribs. "How pale you've gone, Miss Isles – or shall I call you Ruth? Now is that surprise or pure horror?" Ruth shook her head. She felt foolish and gulped the last of her tea. The pleasant high of the leaves revived her enough to hear Vera Blaze amend, "No, I don't mean the town house. Park Row is such a bore. I was thinking of the country place, Blaze House, at Steepacre. It's not twelve miles from St Paul's, so I think somebody once estimated. *He's* off, by the way. Off in Italy with one or two of his more recent mistresses. How lovely. Why don't you pop back to your rooms and pick up what you want for a week or so – I suppose you're free for a week or so? Splendid. Give me your address and I'll send round the carriage in about two hours."

Ruth realized that, having given the address, her lips remained parted. Probably to speak thanks or utter a scream of bewildered joy. Instead she must have, she later thought, sat there like a fish in water as Vera Blaze rose to her impressive height, and stalked, smilingly, away.

Well, she's nearly killed me all right. Now I'll just creep off to my thicket, until she sends her carriage for me and carries me to her lair.

Ruth entertained a vision of a slow devouring by a gold-eyed lioness.

Rather than creep back to her room, she sprang through the streets, as fast as her corset and the omnibus would allow.

Steepacre, when Ruth reached it in the yellow late afternoon light, *was* steep. Everything flowed up or down hill: fields in the first process of producing some sort of grain (corn? wheat?), hedgerows growing in some places to great heights against the thickets of oak trees and coppices of beech. A large village straddled the road with a hump-backed bridge that looked too elderly to be English and was probably Roman. Then the lane showed, through a froth of browning May blossom, the gateposts and the drive. Blaze House rose from its park with an oddly suburban, mock-Eastern look, doorway pillared rather like that of a Hawksmoor church, a little dome balanced above the central roof. For the first time in half an hour, Ruth recalled the city lay, its most bricked and depressing outskirts, just over a rise.

Laurels flanked the door. A huge brown dog with the head of the Anubis jackal-god of Egypt emerged from nowhere and stood staring as the coachman unloaded Ruth's bag. Vera herself had not accompanied Ruth to the house. Apparently she had been delayed and would arrive later and by other means. Nervous already, Ruth had been made less – and more – nervous by Vera's non-appearance. Now the dog compounded her unease.

"He's all right, miss," said a footman in rather slovenly clothing, emerging also from the front door. "He won't do you no harm."

"Really."

"No. Soppy as a duck, he is."

Ruth believed that ducks could be quite dangerous, if roused. But she walked behind the footman and the bag into the house, and when the dog padded in after them, asked, "What's his name?"

"Bacchus," said the footman. After a pause he added, "They all get daft names here."

"All?" Ruth had been pondering who else was present in Blaze's absence.

The footman though only replied that someone would come presently, and then carried off the bag in the upsetting way of such things. The dog meanwhile stood staring again at Ruth.

"Bacchus, here, Bacchus," said Ruth in a firmly courteous voice.

Bacchus turned instantly and trotted away.

The hallway was now what took all Ruth's attention. It was coolly tiled throughout in an Eastern manner, green lotuses and blue and turquoise images of peacocks with gilded tails. A circle of thin pillars needled up to support the roof of the dome two stories above, in which slits of colored glass stained slivers of light like lemons, jade, and raspberry jam. A fountain trickled into a square pool of goldfish.

Of course, it was St John Blaze who had designed the house. Like one of his most luxurious paintings, some Eastern domicile of odalisques... And he called his dog 'Bacchus' and chose his wife for her Russian blood and Russian name. (He had never, Ruth thought, painted her. Or Ruth might never have seen if he had, having never much noticed his paintings even when they were photographed for periodicals.)

A housekeeper came and conducted Ruth upstairs. Curved stairs these were, with gilt handrails that showed spread fans or gazelle hunts, and led to white-washed corridors, and pointed windows covered by lattices of wood that let through only countless diamonds of light.

The room Ruth had been given was also whitewashed, but with a huge plum velvet bed and scarlet settee flung with sequined cushions. An oriental lamp hung down from the ceiling, with a geranium boldly growing in it.

What on earth am I to do here? Ruth thought. But there was also a bathroom, and hot water available. She took a bath and dressed herself in her white evening frock. Outside by then the long yellow afternoon had burned into dark gold. The sun set in a field beyond the tumbling park, catching several woods alight as it fell.

When Ruth exited from her bedroom doorway, she found herself reflected in a mirror. But the wrong way round. She saw herself from the *back*. A startling view. The long white gown, bare shoulders, fair hair scooped up and some left drifting over the neck -

No, it wasn't a mirror, but one more tiled annex, and there inside another girl, in a white frock, standing gazing out of one of the diamond-holes of a lattice.

Who was she?

Ruth hesitated, but then from below she heard the unmistakable voice of Vera Blaze, calling in amused exasperation, "Bacchus! Here, you beast! Good boy! There, your best muddy paws on my skirt. What a *good* fellow you are."

Ruth hurried along the passage.

Like her dog, Ruth thought, now hurrying down the staircase. *Just* like her dog.

Desire, let alone sexual love, disorientates. You might be in the most familiar spot in the world, and if the object of fascination also happens to be there, everything else becomes – not only *un*familiar – but intangible, *oblique*. For this reason, not that of clumsiness or nerves, you drop the well-known cup on the carpet or stub your toe on the door-frame you have successfully negotiated nine thousand and twenty-two times previously. Love is a reinventor.

So now it didn't matter, did it, being in this strange rich man's house, all set about by Moorish tiles and feverish trees, with jackal dogs and backwards-seen mirrored girls. All that mattered was:

"Have a glass of this fruit brandy, Ruth. What a journey. You'd think it would be quite easy, but no. What a fuss they make, men. On and on. Poor chap, he's only twenty-three and acts like some granny in Kiev. Oh we must do this as this. Oh we must never allow that and that—"

It seemed a local neighbor had wanted her to ride down with him in his carriage. Vera had obliged.

"He hopes one day he'll manage an affair with me," she added. "My God, the self-delusion. And I'm old enough besides to be his sister."

Vera was resplendent, having changed into a white silk blouse and burgundy waistcoat over – almost as predicted – loose Turkish trousers. She had also taken down her hair, which ran in dark waters along her back. She smoked one of the cigars, perfuming the (Chinese) drawing room, while Bacchus of the Latin name lay like a sphinx at her feet.

No one else seemed likely ever to come in. Ruth didn't quite dare to say, *Are we alone here?*

As well. Next moment an intruder entered. That was, not a servant, who might be expected to come and go.

Worse, Vera greeted the intruder with a warmed and softened expression, and holding out her hand.

The girl – she was the white-dressed one from the upstairs annex – moved forward slowly.

Ruth felt a flash of deep dismay.

Then Vera said, "Darling, here is a young lady I made friends with in London. Ruth, let me introduce to you my daughter, Emerald."

"Emerald," said Ruth. She heard the disapproval in her own voice. And quickly getting up, nodded to Vera's daughter. "Miss Blaze."

The girl, who Vera was now encircling with an arm, so delicately you could see it was a very *cautious* embrace, turned and looked at Ruth.

No, they were not, Ruth thought, at all alike. Neither she and the girl she had taken for a reflection – nor Vera and the girl who was her child.

It wasn't fair hair she had. Noted in full light, it was like rusty gold. She had a pale exquisite face, modeled maybe from clearest marble. Only her blue-green eyes at all resembled her mother's, in their long, oval, upward slanting. And yet – Emerald.

He must have named her, like the dog.

Even so, she was *well*-named. For her eyes were exactly like that – two beautiful, fabulous *stones.*

"Good evening," said Emerald. She sounded like a mechanical doll. Someone – Vera, by some lightest touch – had turned the little key in her back, and now the girl came to 'life,' and spoke.

Ruth felt horribly compelled, more by curiosity and actual *aversion* than anything else. She crossed the room and held out her hand for Emerald to take and shake a little, in the fashion among worldly women.

But Emerald didn't take Ruth's hand.

"My name is Ruth," repeated Ruth. "I hope I find you well?"

"No," Emerald said at once. "I'm never well. Am I, Mother? Father knows I never am."

"Nonsense," said Vera. But she said it quietly, with a studied playful caution, just like the embrace that anyway, now, she had allowed to drop away. (Ruth let her hand drop too, unshaken.) Then Vera said, "Emily, won't you go into the next room and play us a little music? We'd like that. Play what you want."

"I'll play Papa's favorite."

Emerald moved like an automaton, something graceful on wheels, gliding off into the next section of a room, where a large piano lurked like some black animal.

"Emerald," said Vera, as unearthly strains of Chopin began, "the name's *his* choice, obviously. I call her Emily, once the formalities are out of the way. I ask you. *Emerald Blaze.* It sounds like a race-horse."

Ruth said, "She's very beautiful."

"Beautiful? Yes. If you like something that has no fire in it."

Ruth was herself now quite shocked. She stared at Vera.

"*Is* she your daughter?"

"Mine. She looks more like *him*. She was conceived in a pine forest in Italy, when I allowed him, the first and final time, to have me. It was, our marriage, a mutually beneficial *arrangement*, as you may have guessed. My money, and his – how shall I put this – the *disguise* of being his wife. To begin with he was almost penniless, but already his reputation as a painter grew. My father was on his last legs, poor old fellow. He let me do what I wanted. Blaze and I – it was supposedly a whirlwind courtship. That St John got me with child at once only added to the romantic frisson. I thought of killing it. Something prevented me. When she was born, I knew why I hadn't been able to. I'd never felt love like that. Hadn't been able to imagine it. Emily was my one chance at the normal rights of womanhood. My child? My God, *my child*. And look – look at the state of her."

"What – is it?"

"*What do you think?*"

Ruth felt a flicker of actual fear. Not of Vera – but *at* Vera. Ruth had known she was a tigress, but the tigress now defended her cub.

"Her father," said Ruth.

"Indeed. Her father. But maybe not in the way you think. Let me tell you a story, Ruth Isles. It's one of three that I know about. This perhaps the least."

Ruth sat down on a chair, and Vera, standing up, paced about, every so often returning to fill Ruth's glass with the deceptive, sweet apricot cognac. (The dog lay, head raised and watchful, still.) And all around them, the skeins of the doomed young composer Chopin were glittering and coming apart.

"There is a rumor that Blaze uses the backs and bums of young girls as his mixing table. He does. Sometimes he grinds up colors on their backs, sometimes he liquefies the paint, blending and making exact. Skin, he's told me, is far superior to any wooden palette, or even the ivory palettes of certain old masters. It has, he's said, a *staying* quality – a natural fixative.

"Perhaps you conclude he's done this to me, or to my daughter. Let me instantly disabuse you. He hasn't. I would have cut his heart out if he'd tried that with me. If with her – I would have hunted him with dogs to the coast and killed him in the sea."

(Ruth, her heart galloping, hypnotized. This passion, this protective, astonishing passion – and the inner voice which whispered, under all the outer attention, How could you not love one like *this*?)

"Blaze has almost always picked his models, whether for shepherdesses or Greek goddesses, Arthurian maidens or nuns, from the shoals of the hapless and the needy. Oh, I've seen plenty of them coaxed or dragged into the town house by the back door, bathed and combed and stuffed with food, beer and gin. Drugs too, from the easy laudanum any chemist will sell one, to the burnt black hashish of India. Anyway, after that he can do what he wants with them. He paints them, he fucks them. And some he mixes paint upon. Do you think this is a lie?"

"I've heard – he did that. Mixes the paint."

"Yes. Heard. But I doubt you heard about the results."

Ruth's head swam. She put down her glass. She watched the beloved object of desire, prowling to and fro, her hair lashing around her like the striking tail of a lion.

"There was a woman called Jane Wilkins. He found her in a laundry. Her hands were ruined, he said, but her body was divine. You may have seen the painting – *Phryne at a Window*. An odd compendium of ancient Greece coupled to some sort of renaissance idea – stained glass – trees and leaves – this woman caught by the light. Notice, if ever you see it again, her hands are hidden in her hair."

"I've seen the picture. I remember."

"Then you know. Well, besides painting her, she was one he used as a palette. She was the initial experiment. At first apparently she laughed and said it tickled. Then she liked it. Then she went to sleep. He woke her up to model again while he achieved the first strokes of color on the canvas. Afterwards he sprayed off her skin with oil of turpentine, and then milk, to cleanse. Sent her away with money and her head ringing with wine. This was thirteen years ago. One day, when he was in Italy again, this woman came to me, this Jane Wilkins. She was in a splendid old rage. I saw her in London, in the sitting-room, and before I knew what she was at she'd torn off her clothes and she was naked in front of me. I thought, poor old girl, life's not been kind to you at all. It hadn't. She turned her back, and showed me. What do you think had happened?"

"I don't know. How could I know?"

"I'll tell you, Ruth. Her back – her *back* – the paint had eaten it away, in dappled leprous scars. No, there's no reason such a thing should occur. He'd cleaned it off, I assume, promptly – as promptly as he ever does anything but paint. Or maybe he was rough – or she was, even, trying to clean herself thoroughly. But she was scarred, *dappled*, just like a leper – a leprous leopard. I've a strong stomach, or I'd have been sick. I gave her a lot of money, and of course she often returned for more. But, poor thing, why not. I kept her, you might say, until she died. Do you know how she died? No, as you say, how would you. She was a whore by then and some man, having had her, glimpsed her back. He thought she had syphilis, which she hadn't, so he clubbed her to death and then, blew out his brains."

Next door, along the amber walls drawn with mandarins, Chopin wafted away, began again.

"I see you don't ask me," she said, "his response to the woman's disfigurement or her death."

"Did he have a response?"

"He knew nothing of it. My money, you see, or a great amount of it, is still mine. So long as he receives what he needs, and he's expensive, of course, being a man, so long as he can do as he likes, so can I."

"You didn't tell him."

"Why would I tell him? I've said, there are two other stories I know of, and so does he. Before ever Jane came to me, I'd seen his response to those. Once he said to me, *An artist must have room.* He meant God had made him a genius, so he can do what he wants. I haven't any belief in God, myself. A pity. If God existed, Blaze might eventually burn in hell."

She was far across the long room. Night was settling, deep blue as her former dress, along the windows, lining them. Soon someone would doubtless come to light the lamps and candles. They might even trip over that static basalt shadow of a dog—

Vera swung back through the room, her hair flaring, her eyes igniting from some non-existent fire.

She stood over Ruth, then bending, with a choreographed, non-harmful, couth violence, she gripped the girl's head in her hard warm hands, and kissed her full on the mouth.

Ruth fell into the pool of that kiss. Drunken, released, she looked up into the eyes of her lion-lover.

"Sweetheart," said Vera, "I want something from you."

"Any – thing—"

"No, you can't agree until you know."

"But—"

"My husband is a monster, and he has almost destroyed my daughter. Not in any sexual or obvious way, in any way, for example, some talentless devil in a slum might use – which in fact might be, ultimately, the cause of less injury. He has destroyed her with his deadly presence and his disgusting gift, his obsession with gothic death and classical obliterations. His egoistic thought that women are made, like the beasts of the field, to serve."

Vera bowed her head and kissed Ruth once more, her tongue moving inside the fragrant taste of the brandy, a snake of firm flame. Then, again, drawing back, Vera put her hand gently over Ruth's lips.

"Listen, dear girl. Tell me the truth. What will you do for me?" And the hand, like the seal of a confessional, was lifted.

"Whatever you want."

"Then, my dear friend, I want you to rescue my daughter in the one way I can't – must never – *could* never – do."

"What way is that?"

"*Seduce* her."

TWO

It was Vera I desired. That's obvious enough. And to her daughter – I was frankly averse. That cold, drifting, slightly *crazed* creature, with her red-golden hair and stones of eyes. I'd been glad I hadn't touched her. She would have been chilly, surely, *clammy*, like smooth outdoor marble after winter mist.

And now here I was, walking through the morning rose-garden with her, with Emerald, myself holding a basket into which, now and then, she dropped a forward-blooming rose, perfectly cut, before its hour, by her executioner's blade.

"It seems rather cruel," I said.

I didn't think she would answer. Half the time she didn't. She had never once called me Ruth. But then: "Oh, it is."

"Cutting flowers...?"

"Yes."

"But really, after all they die anyway. It's just these are so young."

"Many die young," she said. "Things, and persons."

The silky rhythm of her voice made me want to slap her.

He has destroyed her, Vera had said.

It wasn't he had ever abused her, either carnally or in the way of physical or verbal unkindness. No – Emerald had always been his darling, when he was at home. And when the demon of painting had him in thrall? "Oh then," Vera had said, "he shut her out of the studio, like the dog."

Apparently she had then sat outside, Emerald the child, on a little chair. She would lay her head on the wall, in order to be able to listen to any movement he might make, or word he might say, more clearly. As his activities in the studio must sometimes have been sexual, I wondered why Vera had allowed Emerald to do this. Vera told me in fact his fornications were rare during the daytime. He preferred to fasten on any model he fancied at night. "He likes darkness for that act," Vera remarked. "Midnight, or a thick forest." And by nightfall, the child was in bed.

When Blaze was not at home, which was very frequently, as his fame soared, little Emerald would pine.

"She did it in such a terrible way. Not sulky or screaming, not bloody awkward and damnably annoying, slamming doors and pulling faces. Oh no. She would be sad. She would wilt. He'd told her, you see, that she was *his* daughter, and that he wished at all times to be made proud of her. He told her what a woman should be, calm, serene, even in sorrow; how she should express herself with soft dignity in her behavior, even in her thoughts."

I had sensed in this Blaze might well have been attacking, by a backhanded route as it were, his forthright, vital, gorgeous wife. But Vera didn't mention that aspect, and nor did I.

From the earliest age Blaze had stroked and molded and suppressed his daughter into what he considered the ideal female icon. My God. Had his notions come from the East, with which he was so greatly – if often inaccurately – involved? Vera suspected this. She had also said, "But in China, they only bind a girl's feet to cripple her. Her mind is allowed some freedom."

Vera had naturally attempted to extract her daughter from this 'benign' tyranny. She had wished to teach Emerald to ride, to swim, to *live*, had tried to take her off to other locations, Florence in spring, and Venice during the Carnival. But Blaze wouldn't go then, though he was often abroad 'alone,' and since Blaze would be in England, Emerald wished only to be there beside him – or even beside the studio wall, listening. Twice Vera had excavated the precious vessel of her daughter from this clinging soil, and whisked her away. "In Rome she almost died of some fever. In Paris she wouldn't eat, and finally fainted in the street, banging her head so badly I had to bring her home.

"She is in love with Blaze. Not sexually. Even that I could grasp, though I would loathe it – it would give me too the rights to separate them. But no, it is this awful 'proper' filial love he sometimes paints. Do you know his picture, *The Dying Sheik and His Daughters*? No. Well, he depicts some desert prince on his deathbed, and these sorrowing lovely wisps of girls clustered round, all dripping with gold adornments and grief-stricken tears. Then there's *Oedipus and Antigone* – the old chap hanging on to a pillar and his frail loving daughter propping him up, all in tasteful Greek drapery. This is what a daughter must be. And as a woman – well, there are all the other paintings for that. The good and lovable women shining with virtue and sweetness, male-worshipping, tender, self-sacrificing. Tennyson's *Lady of Shallot*, *Ophelia* drowned in a madness of loyalty to father *and* lover, *Lucrece*, for God's sake, who kills herself rather than besmirch her husband's honor after her *rape* at the hands of a blackguard. And then there are the evil, distaste-provoking women too. Take a glance sometime at his *Images of the French Revolution*. Some of the ugliest and most ferocious-looking bitches you're likely to see this side of hell."

(Out in the morning garden, Emerald snipped another defenseless bloom, and dropped it in my basket. She was a princess, lost in her own pure, spiritual thoughts, I the servant or slave, a balancing afterthought at the corner of the canvas.)

"So you see, he is killing her," Vera had swiftly said to me the night before, as the Chopin faded again, began again. "Not only by trammeling her, chaining her up in every aesthetic and physical way. He has made her, perhaps only incidentally, obsessed with his gothic imagery – maidens who pine and die, exquisitely, of course, well before their youth and beauty leave them. She isn't solely in love with Blaze. She's in love with death. Let me tell you something else. Less of a story, almost an *anecdote*. One day when he'd been gone a month – she was about sixteen – I went to her room and found she had – how else can I put this – laid herself out, as if for burial. It didn't duplicate one of his studies – but one has sights of these tableaux in his, and other current works. Vases of lilies she'd had them fetch from the hothouse – a white robe – her hair combed over the pillows – her maid had done it, and then, not liking it, come to me. My daughter's hands were crossed on her breast, her eyes shut as if pinned down. I couldn't see her breathe – and for one stupid second I thought she'd taken some poison. Then I stopped being a fool."

"What did you do?"

"Said, It's stuffy in here, and threw up one of the windows. It was a blowy cold March day. She had to get up."

And that was when the Chopin concluded and didn't resume. Emerald Emily came back into the room, and the topic of her mother's and my unbelievable dialogue spun elsewhere. Emerald said very little. We three then had dinner in an Indian dining room of blood-red wallpaper and curtains, against which Vera glowed like a lamp, and Emerald shimmered like vague fading steam.

Hadn't I, and didn't I, at all remonstrate with Vera – if not in those extraordinary moments in the Chinese room? Of course. I was outraged. All the more so because what I wanted had stood in front of me, kissing me to the roots of my spine and soul, telling me I must love – and in such a contrived way – elsewhere. Of course I protested. I said I would leave. (All this after the weird dinner, when every mouthful had threatened to choke me – once did – and I had the infuriating delight of Vera thumping me between the shoulder blades.)

I even said, alone with Vera again at last in a salon – Persian, I think – where she smoked her cigars, that should she not try a more 'accessible' route in the reclamation of her daughter. That was, a young *man*?

"Because surely, Vera," (I was upset enough to be quite brusque with her by then) "if she has been so trained by *him*, a man is all she'll ever want."

"So I'd thought, too," she answered, slowly. "And therefore I have been cultivating young men for her, those of the right type, looks, wealth and so on, for the past two years. Why else do you think I became entangled with that wretched neighbor whose protestations of lust so enervated me on the ride down this evening? But Emily, confronted by even the most winning male, can only compare him to Blaze. Even one she once agreed was nearly as handsome as her father did not, of course, possess her bloody father's *genius*."

"And I," I stated, "possess no genius whatsoever."

"Oh, you," she said, seeming amused again, "you are much more than you say, my girl. The instant I saw you at that peculiar NO charity affair. Why else do you think I sped across like a hungry wolf?"

"I'd flattered myself because the hunger was for *me*."

"It is, my Ruth. But I have to tell you, of all the loves possible to a woman, whether for women, or for men, the love she may feel for her child can gain an incredible ascendancy. Will you – ah, Ruth, for me, as you promised – will you simply try? Only think. If you were to succeed with her, you would have broken her free of him – quite free – and perhaps of all men, forever."

My mother was Sabella Asherton, the actress. She had little time for me and in the end that was mutual. However, having seen her on stage on several occasions, I greatly admired her ability. After her sudden alarming death – she was flung from a speeding carriage at the age only of thirty-four – I never had the resource of complacence to believe I could imitate her skills. Her slowly dwindling little fortune supported me so far, and I was grateful to it. I did much as I liked. These, her only legacies.

Nevertheless, perhaps she left some seed in me of her sparkling theatrical knack, unused till then through all my nineteen years.

Something happened to me in the morning rose garden.

It was very abrupt, without any warning I was aware of. Perhaps I only wanted the little pale monster to stop cutting newborn roses.

I went forward and lightly seized Emerald's left hand.

I did this impulsively, and startled her, too, which *had* been my immediate intent.

Her wide blank eyes stared into my face, her lips slightly parted. She had dropped her scissors.

"Miss Blaze – I can't bear another minute of this!"

No reply, but I did have her attention.

"I must *know*—" I said – what, for Christ's sake, what was I supposed to want to know? "Tell me, please," I said, gazing at her stricken, a player of some small part who has forgotten her lines, longing for the prompt to speak, but the wretch is asleep—

"Tell you? What?" whispered Emerald Blaze, echoing my thought.

Then it came. Oh of course. It was the single possible thing.

"You're *his* daughter," I said, reverently. "St John Blaze. One of the foremost painters of our age. Perhaps in all the world. Tell me *about your father*. I've been dying to know – your mother scarcely speaks of him – and I—"

What a change. A *sea*-change. Great waves washed in, laden with treasure and stars, and her eyes burst alive. While in mine her cool hand warmed and I felt there the faint tick of a pulse.

So *this* was the real key that operated her clockwork. Given what I knew, what else *could* it be? I'd been an idiot not to think of it sooner. To woo a woman I truly didn't want, what could be more appropriate than to beg her to talk about a man I would plainly have detested?

It was a sunny morning. The spread pink buds watched us with shy, malign eyes as we wandered away along the path towards a group of cedars and a summerhouse.

Here we sat down, side by side.

All this while, Emerald was speaking, talking. Not chatter, but a measured musical cadence, utilizing a fair vocabulary and some quite interesting turns of phrase. Once or twice, when I felt I must ask some other (inane) question, she shot me a glance of utter imperious scorn. But when I merely became a sponge, allowing her to choose every facet of the monologue, she was fluent and almost – *affectionate*—

We did not have a conversation as such. However, I *was* permitted – for she seemed to approve of this – occasional soft laughter at her father's witty sayings (of which I recall *none*) or sigh or gasp as his exploits. As for example when he was attacked by bandits in the hills of Tuscany and bought them off by sketching them. A *very* likely tale.

Yet I wasn't bored. I confess it. Partly pride in my own belated cleverness. But also I studied her carefully.

I thought this was an exercise. For I had no intention of doing what Vera had asked of me. It was, I'd reckoned, anyway beyond my ability, aside from any aversion I would feel. Nevertheless I thought I might, now, come at some obscured method I could next impart to Vera, something that, without embroiling myself in unwanted sex with this smoke-wraith girl, might still prove helpful.

I wanted Vera's approval. I wanted to *please* Vera. I wanted her to reward me. (Mercenary little cat that I was.)

Despite all this, watching Emerald, just as the young roses had among their thorns, I did indeed begin to learn other things about her. Although I didn't even know, at that point, that I was. I was so immersed in my acting, for one thing. Which, for a non-professional, wasn't bad at all, though doubtless Sabella revolved in her grave at my ineptitude.

After about three quarters of an hour, Emerald drew breath. In fact she was breathing quite quickly, and pastel color was in her cheeks. She had let go my hand, but now reached for it of her own accord.

"Ruth – would you like to see his gallery?"

"You mean—"

As before she shut me up pretty swiftly.

"I mean I have the key to Father's study. There's a secret door. He showed me long ago. There are sixteen works there – some of them are portraits, some are scenes from legend and myth. Not all have been shown. If you are very circumspect."

I gaped, signaling, in silence, enormous excitement and consciousness of a special treat, plus willingness to slit my veins rather than reveal the hidden trove.

"After luncheon," decided Emerald. "I'll be sent to rest. Then. If you can get away from Mother—" (alas, I knew I could) "meet me in the tiled annex on the second story." It was where I'd spotted her first.

Then, in the middle of my triumph, if so it was, Emerald unnerved me by growing icy pale and lapsing back on the cushioned seat. Was she going to swoon in faultless romantic style? Should I catch her, console her, tell her off?

Again, some new instinct blindly taught me what I should do.

As she fell back, touching her brow, I *copied* her, and I too sank back, closing my eyes in an ecstatic, half-fainting pose.

Even as I did it I was both surprised and, frankly, embarrassed at myself.

But next instant, something astounding.

Emerald leaned to me, smoothed my hands, and drew my head on to her shoulder.

"There, there," she said. "I shouldn't have agitated you so."

And when I unclosed my eyes in total astonishment, her hair brushed into them as she kissed me lightly on the forehead.

THREE

 Luncheon was uninteresting, though it comprised delicious summer dishes and three robust white wines.

"Have some fruit," said Vera Blaze, indicating a mighty horde of forced oranges and peaches.

Ruth selected a peach, Emily declined.

Soon after, Emily-Emerald went to rest for an hour on the couch in her bedroom.

Ruth, seemingly about to emulate her, found herself caught in a sudden furnace of an embrace. "Go, cunning one," Vera said.

It was like being at the beck and call of gods on Olympus.

Reaching the annex, Ruth found Emerald was already there, her face eager and set with certainty.

"You must promise to tell no one."

Allowed to speak? "Yes," Ruth whispered.

"Or," said Emerald, raising her brows, "I should kill you."

Ruth's own eyebrows rose.

In this absurd posture they faced each other. Becoming aware of it, Ruth almost laughed aloud. Instead she looked down, and said, "I never would."

"Swear it," said Emerald.

Held in the dim tiled annex, the latticed diamond lights were littering the floor like debris from a smashed sun.

Ruth put her hand to her throat.

"But—"

"Swear," said Emerald, inexorable as Hamlet's father's ghost.

Ruth said, "By what?"

"By something you hold most dear."

Ruth raised her eyes and was amazed to find she had filled them with water.

"Most dear? That is your father's talent. I swear then, by that."

Emerald smiled.

She was not a lion, nor a lynx. She was – a snake, a serpent, coiled about some apple tree of the heart. She curved her mouth and showed her gleaming flexive wickedness. It had been un-guessable. And was now unmissable.

And somewhere deep in her blood Ruth felt a glimmer like trapped lightning. Scornfully she noted that the emotional sa-dism of Emerald, thinking she had a weaker human being in her grip, was not unarousing.

This damsel had grown up dominated by a patriarchal father, and a powerful mother. It was all she knew – how to be subservi-ent, or, locating a slave more pliable than herself – to *rule*, as she had seen both Blaze and Vera do.

The quality would not have been appealing if turned on some-thing unable to protest – an animal, a servant – but Ruth had already seen that Emerald was wary of the dog, and also of low-flying birds, beetles and spiders in the grass; both polite and re-moved from servants.

Ruth now, however, Emerald seemed to have lured into a per-sonal game. They were female children united in a great secret. But Emerald always being the stronger of the two, the leader, the prince.

So. She *does* have something of her mother.

"There is his study." Emerald pointed. Classical pose, so like a painting. (*Has* he painted her?)

"My God."

"Shush. You mustn't speak. Follow me. Touch nothing. *Look* only."

There was a tall, narrow, dark door, which Emerald unlocked, and inside a large airy study, typical of the room of a rich and un-tidy man who lounged about. Books and old periodicals scattered the scene, there was a cabinet full of statuary, curiously-shaped bottles, pipes, and a stuffed animal in a glass tank that resembled a furious giant squirrel. A desk guarded the way, and leather chairs, and a man's Turkish slippers embroidered with gold lay by the empty fireplace tiled in dragon-green. Oddly – or not – the room otherwise didn't evidence a solitary influence of the exotic East, and where it perhaps showed antiquity, only in a muddled way.

As if he had bought some Greek and Roman artifacts in a job-lot, as some men bought books for their libraries by the yard.

Behind a dusty green curtain, another even narrower door appeared.

"It will only open if I do certain things. You must go through sideways. My father jokes and says Mama couldn't get through, she's too big."

Ha, ha.

"Avert your eyes!" commanded Prince Emerald.

Ruth obeyed.

She heard the door crunch open and only turned and slipped through once her leader had told her she might.

Perhaps it was a secret from the house, but not from the sky. The roof was all glass, as were, Emerald had told her, most of the roofs of Blaze's two studios, here and in London.

Light poured in on an angled walk, on the two white walls of which hung sixteen exhibits, some of which no one else, if the girl was to be believed, had ever seen.

Ruth recognized the first three nevertheless, from reported exhibitions. *Salome's Dance, Ophelia, Girl with a Lyre.*

St John Blaze was, for Ruth, too florid. He did not, she thought, match the purity of a Burne-Jones, nor the adamance of a Rosetti. She didn't care for these sorts of pictures anyway. In art she had always preferred things left more...unsure. Smokier. Cloudy windows barely showing leafy boughs and fruit; ghostly pallid shapes on the edge of life or death.

They moved through the gallery with reverence, Ruth keeping wide-eyed and dumb, while her guide mercilessly detailed every canvas or paper, each element, from charcoal and wash to paint, to types of brush. Even the duration of their making was stressed, sometimes weeks, sometimes months. (Had she timed them all carefully in childhood, leaning her head on the listening wall?)

"This is a sketch of me. My father says he'll never sell it. I told him, if I were to die, I should like a statue made from it, for my tomb."

The voice sounded weaker.

Diverting *herself,* definitely, Ruth gave a little groan and staggered. Emerald turned instantly and caught hold of her.

"I'm sorry. I may die young. Is it so for you?"

In the light-drenched worm of the gallery, they held each other.
Over Emerald's shoulder Ruth saw the little sketch, quite artful
and pleasing. And further along a strange black patch marked
with strips of white – a rug?

"And here," her arm about Ruth's waist, "is the picture of the
poor woman who died from poisoning."

("That," said Vera, some hours after, "is the second story I could
tell you. Do you want to hear?"

Ruth waited. All she really wanted was to sit there, by Vera, on
a red sofa.

Vera said, "A simple matter. I confirmed to you that he used
some of his models as palettes. In this case, the paint ran down
and must have entered the cleft in her buttocks. From where it
was absorbed into her private parts. Apparently neither she nor
Blaze either noticed or objected to this, and eventually she was
washed off by him, like the others. But a week later all her blood
had been poisoned and she died. In agony, so I understand. Her
name was Katie Araby – invented, one assumes."

Ruth thought, wavering, *Do I believe her?* Is she trying to ter-
rify me? *Why?* Does she think I'll do what she wants with that girl
better and more effectively if I am also frightened?

But the waver was solely intellectual. Ruth's senses otherwise
only clamored, like strident gulls, to fall on Vera and be eaten
alive.)

In the early afternoon gallery, things hadn't been that
way at all.

At that time unprimed to the second story of the anally or
vaginally envenomed unfortunate, Katie Araby, Ruth had stared,
missing the painting completely, at Emerald. Ruth did not need to
speak. Emerald preferred still expressive *silences* and wide eyes.

"It was a horrible business," airily said Emerald. "It seems
the girl became impertinently infatuated with my father – and
couldn't control her avowals of love. When he had thrown her

out, she drank lye, or some such ghastly thing. I remember how distressed he was. We spoke of it, of course, only some years later, for at the time it happened I was only a child and it was kept from me. He said that he pitied the poor girl. She had been so unwomanly, loud and unruly – not only in her conduct towards him, but in her manner of dying."

Emerald had stepped away from Ruth, and at the concluding words Ruth lowered her eyes to the floor of the secret gallery, and thought her own harsh tearing thoughts.

Emerald however snapped her back with an abrupt demand.

"You say you greatly admire my father. Perhaps I should ask you, Ruth, to explain yourself."

Emerald's tone had definitely changed. Also she wished Ruth to *speak*.

Ruth raised now gentle but Puritanical eyes.

"His genius makes him godlike to me."

"You're infatuated?" The word she had used dismissively for Katie.

The question too might be one more to be expected from a jealously watchful wife. Ruth said, calmly and humbly, "I believe the gods are best worshipped from afar."

"I see."

Oh, the little brat must have learnt this lordly attitude from her mother. But no – for Vera was not thinly chilly like this. This too must come from Blaze himself.

Nevertheless, where had the floaty swooning maiden gone to? Here was an austere mask of a face, and eyes that were no longer flat polished stones but chips of ice—

"Because, you know," went on Emerald, "my father must never be bothered by that sort of woman again. Not that I think you are that sort. If I'd thought it, I would never have brought you here."

Ruth said, "Emerald, I am socially far beneath all your family. But in the case of your father, I'm worthy only to scatter flowers at his feet, and that in his absence. I really think, if ever I were to meet him – I'd die at once. Like you, I'm not strong. My heart

would never stand it. Like Semele in the presence of Zeus – I'd
burn up and drop in ashes."

Emerald nodded.

She must be addled. Also she was incredibly naïve. Yet even
so.

Even so, I'm enjoying this pretense – this dramatic act I'm putting on.

Once more ashamed of herself, Ruth again hung her head and
Emerald stepped over and took her arm.

They then continued down the gallery, looking at the pictures.
(Ruth wondered, with an inner frown, if any canvas or sketch
here showed Jane Wilkins, the other victim Blaze had indirectly
murdered. She couldn't ask, naturally. Dedicated actress that Ruth
had now decided she was being, the inner frown failed entirely to
reach her surface.)

The sketches, generally, she liked better than the paintings. They
were fragile and in some instances nearly phantasmal – women
in antique clothes, or naked, with long-fingered hands and misty
hair. There was only the one sketch of Emerald, the one she had
said she would like used to model a figure for her 'tomb.' It didn't,
Ruth had privately decided, look at all like her. Perhaps one more
example of Blaze's intransigent creation of the Ideal Daughter,
which even this weird girl had not yet totally achieved.

What intrigued Ruth was, in fact, the peculiar black thing –
not a rug, too small, but perhaps some sort of thick cloth? – with
the white stripes along it. They reminded her of something – she
couldn't think what. She had dared to ask Emerald, in a slavish voice, what it was. And got the disappointment of Emerald's
saying, "That? I don't know. He has never said." "But didn't you
ask?" "Oh, no." "It looks – Egyptian? Moroccan? – some trophy
brought back from there?" But Emerald ignored this and began
another of her lectures on St John Blaze.

Curiously – or was it curious? – as she did this, her sharp de-
meanor melted down in the *blaze* of him, and Emerald became
malleable and soft once more, motivated only by a proper and
discreet daughterly enthusiasm.

Do I tell her mother any of this? Will it help? Surely Vera already knows about these fluctuating twins who are both Emerald?

Ruth became claustrophobic in the gallery, walking endlessly up and down with this mad person clutching her arm and fluting about her filthy swine of a father. Should Ruth fake illness and so get out? Or would Emerald *let* her out? For even now there was a certain bossiness about Emerald.

Finally Emerald did say they should leave the gallery. Too much human presence was not, it seemed, good for the paintings.

What on earth could human presence, Ruth wondered, do to them? It was they, or their maker, who had done harm to *humans*.

They parted in the annex, Emerald embracing Ruth quite tenderly.

"Go back to your room now," instructed Emerald. "In half an hour we must go down for tea. Mother insists on it. She is," observed Emerald, "*addicted* to tea."

So am I, thought Ruth. So are many women.

"Is your mother—" said Ruth, cautious, "that is – she seems strict with you—"

"Oh, what do I care? She's nothing to me," said Emerald, and the mask face was there again, a fleeting hard second.

"But she is your mother."

"Well, perhaps *your* mother is very lovable to you," said Emerald. Landing, had she known it, a perfect hit. Touché.

And so on to the passion-red sofa, where Ruth sat with Vera, after Emerald had vaporized away from the teapot and the cigars.

"I can't do this, Vera."

"Yes, you can, Ruth. Haven't you seen the alteration in my daughter? I can see it. She has some life flowing in her pale veins."

"That is *his* life. She is only interested in *him*."

"And weren't you clever to make believe that you were too."

At least Vera didn't, for a moment, mistake Ruth's lies to Emerald, which she had recounted in a combination of disgust and actorish pride.

But then Ruth spoke to Vera of the canvas of the woman who had been 'poisoned.' And Vera put down her cup, scowled magnificently, crossed her legs – whose shape was clearly visible through another pair of Turkish trousers, long, muscular and leonine – and told Ruth the facts of the death of Katie Araby.

Vera then said, "My child showed you his odd little gallery, into which I'm supposed never to be able to penetrate. So, now I'll show you the hothouses. Would you like that, my astonishing Ruth?"

Ruth said she would.

She had been galvanized by the addictive evil tea. (How many knew that the famous tea-totallers had been of two sects – one which would drink tea and never alcohol, *one* that had determined to destroy the impact of tea leaves, or at least stop incorrigible females from supping the devilish brew.) She sped out with Vera, laughing. They too went arm in arm, like comrades going on some jaunt, or to a glorious just war, of which they had no fear.

I'm in love with her.

Ruth, *no*. Don't be.

Don't.

Too late.

How apposite, Vera's choice, also: the hothouses. (There were three – it was like an embryonic Kew Gardens.) Ribbed glass roofs provided accommodation for twenty-foot palm trees, pineapple vines, primeval ferns, and succulent stems the color of magenta sugar. They were hot and steamy, with the occasional gardener bowing like a reed before Vera's progress. Appetizing in the extreme.

Oh drag me wildly into the arboretum or the olifernery and smother me with your hands and mouth—

Ruth giggled at her ideas.

Vera chuckled, smacked her hand lightly (mind-reading?), and picked for her a crimson orange. "Eat this. We will come to other things presently."

The Garden of Eden. A non-present God, whose disposition was sane and not unkind. Adama and Eva. Innocent, lustful. Who would have cared about Knowledgeable Apples? Who wanted them, if you could have – this?

But shades of evening drew on across the gardens, smoking the conservatory glass, and in the house on the rise, lights were igniting. Dinner must occur, like a dreadful unpreventable accident. Emerald the Serpent would waft to the table and coil about them.

"Vera, truly – I can't—" for the first, Ruth heard the forlorn desperation in her tone.

"Hush. I've seen you can."

Night falls on Paradise. The angel with the flaming sword has cruelly lit all the lamps.

Dinner. The accident had certainly occurred. A cow, a sheep, a fish and several potatoes, lettuces and eggs, had been involved.

Ruth watched Emerald surreptitiously. Yes, there *was* a change. A faint pastel – excitement? – radiated from her.

And though she kept up the mannerisms, charming or infuriating depending on who beheld them, of decorous frailty, you began to notice a spine of steel holding all the fluttering together.

A snake.

Ruth had a headache. The wine made it worse.

She knew what had caused it. It was desire unfulfilled. Vera, for heavens sake. And after all, to be *used* like this. It was unfair and in bad taste. And, thought Ruth, belligerently at her *most* mercenary, would she receive her sexual wages at the end of this palaver? Probably not. Vera was an empress who employed her, that was all. There would be some humiliating debacle with the girl, and from Vera a kiss and a pat, and maybe, if Ruth had *really* tried to seduce – had even succeeded – with Emerald perhaps screaming with affront and dashing out howling into the house to alert all the servants – a payment of some sort, some trinket, or even money. *I shall spurn it.* Angrily Ruth amended, No, I'll take it. I'm not so rich I can afford to be honorable too. *Damnation.*

Emerald murmured, "Does your head ache?"

Ruth realized she had been smoothing her own forehead absently. "Yes." Too brisk. "I'm afraid it does," she docilely appended.

"It's the candles. Mother has so many lit. And her wretched cigars. I can even smell them up in my room sometimes."

"I don't dislike—"

"No, if a *man* smokes, it's quite all right," said Emerald.

They spoke *sotto voce*. Emerald had drawn her chair somewhat nearer to Ruth's, Ruth indifferently noted.

Vera meanwhile had grown more distant, in a complementary mode. Ruth, her temples pounding, saw Vera as if from the wrong end of a telescope.

The dessert was being served. Ruth felt queasy.

She stood up. "Lady Vera, please excuse me. I'm afraid I have a very bad headache and must lie down."

Vera smiled. Having been told of the ploy of feminine weakness, now she took truth for lie.

"Of course, my dear. Please ring for one of the maids if you find you can't sleep it off. They keep busy until midnight, and Emily has some excellent drops. You won't mind that, will you, Emily?"

"No, Mama," said Emerald, lowering her eyes like half-sheathed green daggers.

Ruth forgot to say good night to Emerald, or Vera. She felt now quite ill and went out slowly. Unlike the Serpent, Ruth hated to be at any physical low ebb. It made her self-conscious and vulnerable, and neither feeling appealed.

She went upstairs also slowly, and once paused, to rest her shrieking head on the cool of the gazelle-littered brass banister. Raising it again she saw, through the blur of lights. Emerald had come out, and looked up at her, with the most delicate unkindness of a look the affronted Ruth had ever seen. But Ruth was past caring. She floundered to her room in bad-tempered physical misery, flung off her clothes and lay down on the bed, nursing some oil of lavender, with every candle blown out.

FOUR

I had slept about four hours. Somewhere an eerie clock was chiming. I counted the strokes through the swansdown of confusion – one, two, and then, after a slight delay, three.

So it was three in the morning.

I tested my headache, which had gone, leaving only a muddy emptiness. But I was outraged, depressed.

Everything smelled of lavender, that lovely light mauve aroma, comparable only to the intensest marzipan.

Only about an hour to dawn. I turned my head on the pillow to sleep a little longer, and exactly then heard a noise against my bedroom door.

This was always the problem with servants. (I had none.)

What could they possibly want?

"What do you want?" My voice sounded feeble. Anyone with any strength of character would totally ignore it, and stamp straight in.

Sure enough, the door opened.

And in my mind, another voice spoke: *At last.*

At last? My God – had Vera decided to give me – something on account?

In the dark, nothing was at all visible. And then there came the hottest gleam. A struck match.

I couldn't see. But in the blinding light, felt someone bend over me.

A scent of melon (the hothouse?) and of – not cigars – *cigarettes.* Tailored cloth, cologne, *tobacco*—

I forced my eyes to open. And flung myself upright on the bed.

The match had lit both a cigarette and a single candle. A young man stood there.

"Get out!" I exclaimed. Sounding, to myself, like some imbecile. "How dare you—"

"Oh, I *dare*," said he. It was a light, blond voice. And then he gave a boyish laugh. "Do you know me, little girl?"

I lay back on the pillows, astounded, clad – as I was well aware – in only a light summer nightgown, my hair loose, and nothing defensive to hand save a bottle of lavender oil.

And then.

"But you are—" I faltered.

"Who do you think I am?"

I knew. It wasn't Vera. This was her daughter, dressed up in an elegant grey jacket and trousers, in a lawn shirt – in a man's daytime clothes. Her long hair was tied back. She gave the impression of a thin, beautiful young fellow, about sixteen, decadent, and full of juice.

My wits were reassembling and I said, carefully, "I don't know who you are. Who are you?"

"Of course you know. Do you think I look like him?"

Who? Oh. Who else. Yet how could I tell, I'd never knowingly even seen a photograph of her father.

"Yes..." I breathed.

"Yes," she agreed. "And only I have this privilege, for I am the only woman able to copy him, I am half of him. And I am *very* like him. Aren't I? St John Blaze. Say it, Ruth. Say *St John*."

Something caught me. I crooned, very low, "I can't. I cannot be so familiar."

Again that *boyish* laugh. She said, "Well, you're a find, ain't you? What then?"

"Sir St John," I muttered, well conscious of the unwieldy phrase.

"All right," she said, "you may call me simply Sinny. Quantities of my girls do that. Say it then. Sinny."

I gritted my teeth. "Sinny," I said.

The thought ran about in the back of my brain, while the foremost part of my mind only struggled with her appearance and her sudden arrival. The thought of how she had devised this overly reduced quaint title. Had she *heard* as much, through the wall when, as a child, she listened? *Call me simply Sinny.*

It was marvelous really. She did look male, although perhaps too beautiful for that – save in some masculine circles, such beauty might have been more than acceptable.

I lay there, staring.

She said, "You're much too audacious, my naughty Ruth. You said you worshipped him," (had I? Never.) "and so, if I'm his avatar, you must worship *me*."

She'd become her father, but *I* didn't know what to do. But I had *nothing* to do. My speechless amazement was apparently enough.

She leaned over me, and I caught again the scent of her, between female and male. Were these clothes *his*? Surely she was too slight of build to wear his apparel – she must have had them made – but she had used his colognes and unguents.

And the cigarette, probably, was one of his best.

"Do you love me?" she said.

"You are my god," I said. (Thank you Sabella, mother mine, for the prompt.)

But there was that about Emerald now, it was quite easy to fawn on her. *Want* her. *Did* I?

It was not the manly pose, God forbid. It was the power she had derived from it.

I knew she must have done this several times before. She was practiced.

I knew too both I – and Vera – had been preempted and overruled.

"If you think I'm your god, then you must let me use you," she expounded on her theme.

"Yes," I said, "Sinny."

"Or," she said, "I may change my mind."

What melodrama.

I'd have liked to push her out of the room.

But instead I let her mouth come down on mine.

Without doubt, as I said, she had done this many, many times before. In fact I had the sense she had done it since the time of Lilith – since the very Eden I had witlessly visualized for myself and Vera.

Her tongue fondled my teeth and gums, slid backward to the roof of my mouth, seeming to enter my nose, my eyes – a snake's tongue – blinding, tickling, bewildering me—

Arousal came in an intense leap.

Before I could stop myself I took hold of her.

"You're bad," she said, lifting her mouth. "A bad woman." (Had she heard this through that wall? Obviously he *had* had women then, by day, he must have done, or how else did she know?)

"I love you," I lied. Feeble. I should loathe myself tomorrow. But that wasn't yet.

The lie was sweet. I knew she would, as Vera hadn't, reward me.

Emerald lowered herself and knelt over my body. She folded up my nightgown, then bending her head, put that warm honey mouth first onto my right, then my left breast.

All the lust I'd felt before, unappeased, flamed into renewal.

A voice in my head warned me, If you cry out, remember she's – she's – *Sin*—

But a wiser voice said, Now protest, deny.

"Don't," I moaned, "please spare me."

"Bitch," she said. Her fingers slipped inside me, as her tongue played my breasts. Her thumb twitched nimbly on the piquant clitoral nub.

Before I could know what my body was at, I spasmed an intense brilliant flicker, like strong summer lightning. At my gasps, she thrust her velvet tongue again into my mouth and nearly into my throat, throttling me.

I lay dead beneath her. Vanquished.

I thought, Pretend to be sorry. So I sniveled.

"No," she said, Emerald Sinny. "Now you must turn onto your belly."

And that was when panic stirred far down, in my core that craved only the briefest rest, to be followed by more of her attentions. And Panic said, Now she'll treat you as *he* does his girls. *The Palette.*

Do you want paint mixed on you behind your back?

When Vera came into the breakfast room the following day, I was sitting upright as a poker, and ready for battle.

I knew there must be one. I didn't look forward to it, caught between a need to offend her and another need to placate. I thought too she wouldn't believe me, for she'd closed her eyes to it all anyway. I could hardly think a woman of her intelligence and caliber could remain in such total ignorance, except through the process of self-deception.

Emerald had not come down. I seized the moment as Vera stood there, levelly eyeing alternately myself and the cuts of bacon on the sideboard.

"I must talk to you as soon as possible."

"Yes?" she asked, with that idle teasing grace of hers. "Then of course."

I tried to bite back rioting words, but heard myself declare, "You won't like a word of what I have to say."

"Dear me. Should I tremble?"

"You should prepare yourself."

"My dear Ruth, you begin to sound like a heroine from one of the novels by the Misses Brontë."

The door was opened by the slovenly footman.

Both Vera and I braced ourselves visibly – she certainly did, and I am sure I must have done – for the advent of Emerald. But it was the Anubis dog who entered and padded quietly across the room to lie down by the terrace doors.

Then a maid bustled in. It seemed Emerald begged to be excused the breakfast. She was enervated and had elected to stay in bed.

Vera raised her brows. Her lips turned down.

When the maid had gone again and shut the door, Vera said to me, "Something has happened." I said nothing. Vera said, "I assume not what we hoped—" (*we* hoped—) "would happen? Or have you succeeded?" She looked, contrary to her words, grim enough.

"In a way," I said. "She came to my room."

"*She* came – to *your* room – you mean you invited her there?"

"No. I woke up and found her there, lighting a cigarette."

"A – what can you mean? She doesn't smoke. She can't abide it when I do. Even her beloved father's cigarettes make her dizzy."

"Vera," I said, "she isn't what you think. Or what *she* thinks, possibly, half the time. Your daughter is a deceiver, Vera. To others and to herself. She is a sort of fiend, and worse than a fiend—" I felt my face grow hot with anger to match the rage I saw bloom in Vera's. This wasn't how I had planned to tell her. I said, "Forgive me. Let me recount everything in the proper order. Will you listen, and agree only to attack me when I've finished?"

Her eyes were like broken suns, splinters of burning threat; her voice was icy. "Go on," she said.

FIVE

The girl who had become a young man stood over Ruth, playful and menacing, and Ruth thought the best, thing would be to get up at once and thrust the intruder out of the door.

Lust had sunk to a dry tingling; curiosity had grown more insistent.

Deciding, Ruth turned her now-naked body over on the bed. She lay in waiting. Ruth was strong. If she had to, she could escape Emerald, and almost certainly subdue her. Ruth kept her right arm ready, folded across under her breasts, all prepared to lever herself upward and away.

"You have a nice back," said Emerald, in a professional tone. "Broad here and here – slender here. The corset marks have almost faded. What ugly things you women wear, don't you, to please us?"

Something silken stroked along Ruth's spine. Was Emerald preparing to lash her with some scarf? But no, it was only the tied-back coil of Emerald's long hair pouring forward. Then Emerald's hand and mouth began to work on Ruth's back.

What heavenly pleasure. The hands moving with a firm sliding, the tongue following, describing each muscle and vertebra.

There was no fulsome wetness, no paint involved – was there? Ruth, though she could not see, thought there was not. The warm wet tongue, the silky hair, were the only brushes, and the stroking hands the only palette knives.

But had it, for those women he mixed his colors on, felt at all like this? Perhaps...

"They all like the procedure," said Emerald in a drowsy amused voice. "Even the ones who thought they wouldn't, and protested. And nothing bad came of it. Save just three times."

Ruth felt Emerald climb up on to her buttocks. The girl weighed very little, and sitting astride Ruth, Emerald began to ride. Sensually alerting as this was, Ruth was now well aware that such a bow-legged stance would be insupportable for an eighteen-year-old woman who had never done it in the past. This girl who had refused to learn to ride a horse had, nevertheless, loosened the joints of her thighs on other gallops.

Emerald began to make sounds, little rough *mmms*, and next short rasping grunts. She clutched Ruth's hips, rubbing her centre against Ruth's body so now Ruth felt on her the tinselly moist scratch of pubic hair. The trousers were undone then, and (obviously) no male equipment had spilled out. *But she is still, isn't she, mixing her colors on my back?*

Ruth had supposed from the prelude Emerald might be noisy in climax. But in fact at the peak, all sounds ended, apart from a high thin whining note, like a whistle blown miles off.

Emerald dismounted, and lay down. Ruth turned her head on the pillow with an undeniably amorous interest, and saw the pale face full of the flame of recent orgasm, the eyes shut and lips taking drafts of air.

Emerald said, "Yes, look at me if you like. But you didn't see me when it happened. Did you?"

"No. I should have liked to..."

"Well, that isn't the bargain, my dear," said Emerald, her female loins gleaming dull gold in the candle-flicker, her masculine persona adroit and present. "I'll only take you in the dark, or from behind, or both. You'll never see."

So *that* was St John Blaze's taste. Ruth accepted it had been apparent enough. A man who didn't like a woman to watch his moments of ecstatic weakness – or, maybe also, to witness hers, face to face.

Ruth lay along Emerald's body, watching her now sidelong, her head on her arm.

The candle was fading. Soon it should be dark enough – for *Sinny* – but morning was also close, already the bloody birds were squeaking and trilling from the garden trees.

When Ruth reached out, gently to caress Emerald's body, Emerald stiffened and pushed her hand away. "Don't be greedy, Ruth."

At that moment Ruth's patience – if that was what it could be called – snapped.

"Only once then? Aren't you good for more than once, *Sinny?*"

"I'll show you what I'm good for when I'm good and ready."

Ruth sat up. "Perhaps not." It was worth a try.

And indeed Emerald – or *St John* – reacted, sitting up too. But she – he – *they* – only let out a laugh – that laugh of a boy.

"I'll tell you a story. Shall I? Will that cool you down?"

This is all my own fault, thought Ruth. She bit her tongue which *Sinny* had married with her-his own.

Emerald got off the bed. She moved away, and blew out the candle suddenly with a snake's hiss.

The thick curtains really did contain a little light, like a thinness wearing in the fabric of darkness. But Emerald had become only a blot of shadow. Ruth realized her own nakedness would show more vividly, and with fresh twinges of unease, she pulled the red coverlet up around herself, to hide.

"I killed three women," said Emerald, said Sinny. "Of course, you'll acknowledge I never meant to." (Dear Christ, had he said this – if not to his child, then where his child could overhear?) "There was one woman who became scarred and later I heard, in a roundabout way, some fellow shot her. Or did he brain her? Can't recall. Another – this was mentioned to you – died of poisoning. I think my dear little girl excused me by saying the woman drank lye. But in fact it was the confounded paint – tartar of quicksilver and yellow ochre, I'd deduce. Went into her crack. The third fatality though, that was a queer do."

Ruth's sexual glimmerings had gone out like the candle in the breath of these words.

She was already glad she hadn't been able to have Emerald Blaze again.

"You see," said Sinny, "she was a blackie. A whore from a brothel up Hyde Park way. Specialty of the house, she was. They called her by some outlandish name – what was that? Oh, yes, Thubeah. I bought her for an evening, not for sport, but to paint."

(He was in the room. St John. Telling Ruth the third story. Telling it with a boy-girl's voice, regretful, a touch, mostly fascinated at the eccentric flare of his artistic life.)

"I wanted this black whore for a canvas. A Nubian slave woman. You can see it, the composition, if you go to the National Gallery. *Hecuba and Her Women*. Some pedantic fool said they didn't keep Negroes in Troy, but artistic license, old man. Wonderful, the effect of that blue-blackness in the corner, behind the other cowering rosy girls."

Sinny left off. In the half-dark half-light, (where light surely must, by now, be winning over dark, but was not) Ruth saw the sulphur shot of another match. Sinny had lit him-herself a second cigarette.

"I had an inspiration," said Sinny, thoughtfully. "I'd seen a zebra skin, all the way from Africa. They're striped black on white, but here was this other animal, and My God was she black – quite pretty in her way, though less so than a monkey or a cat. And I thought, how about *white* on *black*? So, when I'd done the other stuff, I painted her, her back, you understand. She said, in some bizarre accent I can't begin to imitate, What are you doing? I said, Mixing a color, Thubeah. I often do this. Skin makes a wonderful fixative, even yours."

Another silence.

Then: "I worked very hard that night, exhausted myself actually – slept a whole day after. Of course I didn't want to touch her in other ways, the blackie. I fell asleep too in my studio chair. When the servant woke me, she had gone. It seemed her keeper had come, from the whorehouse. That was the deal, after all. It seems she didn't know I'd painted white stripes on her black back until others saw and laughed, and told her."

Ruth sat, clutching the coverlet. She thought of the black woman, perhaps royal in her own country, as had been a black actress who had sometimes worked at Sabella's theatre. She thought of her made into a slave, a sticking-place for white men. And finally made into one man's exclusive canvas.

Ruth said, quietly, "That was what the black and white cloth on the gallery wall came from, was it? He painted her, then made a painting from the design he'd made on her?"

"No, it didn't happen like that. You see, if you'd talk less and listen more, you'd get the facts much quicker. Thubeah went mad in her brothel, after she saw the white stripes on her back. Why? Who can say how the mind of such a woman – let alone a savage – works."

"Who can say..." echoed Ruth.

She felt tears run down her face, and bowed her head, in case the lit cigarette or the slow rise of dawn might reveal them.

"She hanged herself," added the story-teller. "I'd paid to have her cared for by then. Had to. They made a great fuss, and some most unreasonable threats – their specialty of the house spoilt for them, similar rubbish. So when she was found dead – well, the physician who cared for her was a pal of mine. I'd done a most flattering portrait of his stout wife for him, gratis."

"You took some of Thubeah's skin."

"I cured it, and put it up on my wall. Oh, it's macabre, I grant you, so I've never been too public with it. But it has a fine pattern, you see. If you look, you'll find that pattern reproduced by me, here and there, in other canvases. Strangely inspiring, I found it."

Silence once more.

Ruth said, "Does your daughter know, Sir St John Blaze?"

"Christ, of course she does. Knows all her Papa's escapades, my little Emerald. It's nice to have a woman to talk to sometimes, the right sort of woman. Not Vera, I have to say. She knows next to nothing about me, I can tell you."

"Then why," said Ruth, "if she knows, did Emerald say she *didn't* know?"

"Oh, she thinks she don't, if you like. She's very ladylike, my girl, a proper womanly woman. She *thinks* she doesn't know a very great deal. Getting light now," he added. "Better get back to bed before that great ox Vera catches us. Thanks for the merry time, Ruthie. You're a good bad girl."

Naturally the dawn would not enter the room until he – she – that *entity* had left it. How sensible, the dawn.

Ruth sat in darkness and in darkness heard it stride out of the door, leaving behind only the trail of smoke, and the reek of hell.

"This is absurd," said Vera, when Ruth had finished her account.

Ruth's face was high-colored and taut, Vera's pale, almost brooding. She spoke still without heat. She seemed to be interviewing it all over again, even as she denied its likelihood, *thinking*, questioning – not only Ruth's memories from the previous night – but her own from the past.

Ruth now kept quiet. She prickled with shame and distaste. She didn't know, as they said, 'where to put herself.'

Vera said, "How does she know that story – about the poor black girl? She must have eavesdropped – he'd *never* have told her. It's only gossip anyway, may not even be true."

Ruth couldn't maintain her quietness.

"Did you ever doubt it? Haven't you ever seen the piece of black – *skin* – on the wall of his private gallery, marked with white paint?

"No." Vera picked up her cup and set it down again without sampling it. "Tell me, what happened after Emily left you this morning?"

"I lay down and watched the daylight come."

"You see," said Vera. "I ask particularly, because of that maid who announced just now my daughter would stay in bed this morning. This maid and I have a certain code between us for Emily's activities and moods. From how she phrased her message, I assume my daughter's again *playing dead*." Ruth jumped. "Yes, stretched out between vases of funeral flowers and her hands crossed on her bosom. How can that be, if last night anything of what you say happened, did so."

Ruth said, hesitantly now, "But of course it would. He – Blaze – made her into this little pliable fragile maiden from one of his paintings – but *she* – she wants not to be a maiden at all – *she* wants to be *him*. Maybe it began innocently enough, when she was a child. She missed him so much when he was away, all she could do, other than demonstrate herself his faultless daughter, was to copy his presence for herself. Someone probably had said to her how like him she was...is she? I assume she is?" (Vera said nothing now.) "Or maybe she noted a likeness for herself. So she became Blaze, for herself in the only fashion possible. By becoming what he was. And is. And now she continues to act the role of her father. While at other times – Vera, Emerald is trying to kill off the part of herself that is the *female*. Oh not literally – even she sees if she really dies, they *both* do. So it must be symbolic. And once Emerald's properly, spiritually dead and buried, then she'll only have to be one person: St John Blaze."

Vera got up. "Then she's mad."

"Perhaps. Or worse."

"How could it be *worse*?"

"Because I think, though she is doing all this, she is horribly sane."

"Be silent!" The roar of temper was powerful, like a slap. "This is my daughter we are talking about."

Ruth too rose. She said, "I've packed my bag. I can walk to the station – I gather there is one, at Steepacre Hamlet."

"Don't be stupid. It would take you three hours."

"I have been stupid, Lady Vera. I have allowed you to use me, and all we've achieved is more distress, and a most repellant certainty. As for time," said Ruth, her heart hammering, her mouth thin as a thread, "we seem to have wasted such a lot of each other's already, what will three more hours matter to me?"

The dog lifted his head, in an inquiring way. But Vera did not argue or attempt to restrict. She let Ruth walk from the room, and presently from the house.

It was a bright-feathered, glittering day, full of promise. For some.

Extract from a letter sent by Melisande (née Mabel) Crabtree to her friend, Lydiana (née Anne) Blenkinsop. Dated approximately one year after the preceding chapters.

It is, as I say, dear Lydiana, sumptuous here. Such a shame you could not join us. There can be no country to compare with Italy. Unless, perhaps, Greece, or France. Or Spain. Or England, in summer. Or apparently Upper Germany is quite a picture. Or the Himalayas, wherever they may be. Meanwhile I *must* relay some gossip I heard of a mutual – I cannot say friend – actually the daughter of Lady Vera Blaze, the wife of the great artist, who, as you know, I am acquainted with. My goodness! Such a scandal! It seems Emerald Blaze is now living in a villa just outside Rome, surrounded by ancient artifacts and young women of all types! She has long declared them her HAREM. (The women, of course, not the artifacts.) She lords it over them all, dressing in male attire, and even, so I am reliably told, affecting a small mustache – which surely must be glued on, for how could she *grow* such a thing? It appears she first arrived in Italy, as she *said*, in flight from her 'termagant mother' – that dear Lady Vera, who is so elegant and charitable – Do you know, she once donated TWO GUINEAS for some beads at a stall I was operating for the Northern Orphans – And then she, Emerald, fell into a decline in Italy. They *say* she is supposed to have *died* – or at any rate, been *buried* – truly BURIED – in an open grave out on some hillside. And in the morning – how dreadfully blasphemous – she came back to life. Her horde of females next led her down the hill, and from then on Emerald has become, and remained, 'male.' Her name, or so my source (I dare

not reveal *her* name) avows, is *Emidio*. She – should I
say *he*? – speaks such fluent Italian that everyone thinks
her – him – a young Roman count. *And* a *man*. Who is
scandalous only in having so many women at his house.
I may add that, here, to have not only a wife, but three or
four mistresses, is considered quite abstemious. But, my
word, what can her father think of her, that great painter,
Sir St John Blaze? No one knows what goes on *there*,
although again, my source (I will confess more about *her*
at a future date) tells me Sir S. turned up at the villa,
whereat his daughter – the mustachioed Emidio – *fired a
gun at him*! Point blank, from a window. The bullet only
took off his hat, it seems. But in the village everyone took
Sir S. – for *Emidio*! They are now, apparently, so alike.

I must now consign this to the postal service, of which,
its being Italian, I have little hopes. You will doubtless
not receive a line for several days.

EPILOGOS

Vera reentered my life three years after I had first
met her. I'd been dragooned into helping at some
book-stall, I can't, even vaguely, remember why,
but abruptly there she was.

Three years had changed nothing, only accentuated her powerful lioness allure. Although she *had* lost her name, having di-
vorced her husband, the famous painter, for adultery – which he
had allowed. There she stood, in a dark green costume, under a
wheel of hat, staring down her lion's nose at me.

My knees and my wrists dissolved, my eyes said everything that
must never, ever, be said by the voice in public.

"Here you are," she exclaimed, off-hand, as if we had been
parted only half an hour and she had been looking for me. She
stared next, imperious, at the other woman who was tending the
stall. "Do take over, Daphne. Miss Isles and I simply must have
a cup of tea."

The teapot secured (it was a winter season, a London through the window sooty and full of rain, but oh, now burning like the Great Fire of 1666), we sat and talked for two hours.

To this day I can't recall what was said, at least not much of it in actual dialogue. It was like a piece of exquisite music, a duet I had always wished to play, and now at last a golden piano sounded, and a violin of stars was put into my hands, and I became, as she was, a virtuoso.

"My daughter," she did add, as we got up, and this I *do* recollect, "she has long removed herself from my life. I will say nothing of my feelings about that. Such things, like memories of the surgeon's knife, are better left to decay. Therefore, we will not speak, from this moment, a single word of her."

"Never," I said. Though, years after, one other thing was said, of Emerald – but at this moment it had and has no place.

"I wronged you," said Vera, with such dignity I saw only guilt had caused it.

I answered, "I loved *you*."

"I'm glad, my Ruth... Ruth... Doesn't that mean 'Pity'?"

"No. It means love."

"And what about these wet grey streets?"

"Love."

"I have another house now. At Richmond. We can lounge about there and drink tea and smoke – and, my girl, if you'll visit me there, no one will interrupt. Except perhaps the old dog, Bacchus. You didn't mind him, did you?"

"No. He was yours."

"He's a gentleman. I tell you the truth, Bacchus sometimes reminds me of my father. One of the few fine men I have ever known. I once vexed Blaze very much by telling him how, if more men behaved with the honesty and discretion of Bacchus, the world would be a better place. But then. No more of bloody Blaze now, either. I've become again simply Miss Vera Tresky. Do you like that at all?"

"Yes. I like it more than I can say."

And so we went to Richmond.

It was a fine old house that overlooked the reedy river, one silver spoon-like sweep. In the boating-house lay a new boat. Sometimes we would row out to a small island, leaving the dog behind, (since otherwise he would disturb our love-making, having wild interests in the ducks and swans).

Did Vera then, afterwards say anything more about her daughter, the daughter she so loved that she'd never been able to imagine such love beforehand? Only on one occasion. Vera murmured then to me, between sleeping and waking, in a sort of dream, that St John had been unbearable enough. His replica, in the form of her daughter – Vera must then have seen the apparition, too – had at first nauseated, then carved deeply into her (the knife she had mentioned?) thereafter – and is this the strangest or most reasonable? – had no interest for her. She shocked me, when I heard her say this. Or, not so much shock at her, more shock at what life brings us to. For I knew by then how much Vera had adored and cared for the well being of her child: she had given me up to Emerald, and might have lost me. I knew by then also you see, I was not alone in the state of love.

Aside from this, over the years, I heard one or two things independently of Emerald Blaze. For one, that she'd tried to shoot her father through the head at some spot near Rome. This seemed not so far-fetched to me. For if she had by then *become* entirely St John Blaze, and legend had it this was so, he was finally redundant. Even, perhaps, a rival.

A last note I must (reluctantly and churlishly) add. I have seen a canvas which Emerald – or 'Emidio' – subsequently painted. It is called *Three Muses*. A weird work, and not *very* well done, getting the slight attention it did only because of the peculiar circumstances of Emerald's later life. The muses are shown, each from the back. One is very pale-skinned and dappled oddly, like a leopard, one is more ruddy – as if her blood were not wholesome. One is black, with a jagged white striping, as if she had been lashed to the bone.

I never mentioned any of this to Vera. Nor, if she knew of it, did she relay any of it to me. Generally she had been right. It was better, definitely, that we didn't speak of Emerald Blaze.

Vera and I knew each other always, from the day of our re-meeting, and lived often in each other's company. We traveled, too – Bacchus is buried in a wood near Athens – the Midsummer Night Wood, Vera called it. He lived to be almost eighteen. A heroic age for a dog, though for a woman very little.

Even now I've grown old, I can't bring myself to speak much of Vera's own death, though it was peaceful. She was by then well over seventy, and I, at the time, an elderly woman in the prime of her sixties. Nor, as you see, do I speak much of our relationship. We were never especially faithful to each other. Which never mattered. Something stronger than sexuality stayed between us until the day she left me forever. Something, dare I say, even stronger than love.

Age

Judas Garbah

We were dining together, Miche and I, in a small restaurant near the Moulin Rouge. There was nothing between us. Really neither of us had anyone else just then to have dinner with.

Outside the night was loud with car horns, voices and lights. The dark restaurant was russet from food and smoke. The candles burned in yellow clumps.

Across from us, a noisy blonde woman, overweight and thick with paint, was making a display of her meal. The waiters fluttered round her obsequiously, then went off and sniggered at her in corners. Over the back of her little chair, quaking at her weight, was carelessly draped her white fur wrap. "And those are diamonds in the fat bitch's ears," said Miche. "They should throw her out, the fat sow. My God, at her age, that rouge, those lashes – and the voice of a crow."

Through the cover of the smoke I'd been watching her. I was ravished by her, frankly. She ordered this and that, was courteous, brisk, bubbling, appreciative, haughty. Then flirted with her lined, lead-heavy eyes, smiled her red lips over teeth too long and stained by forty-five years of good cigarettes.

"Judas, don't look at her like a sheep. She knows what *we* are, don't worry. You didn't see her glare as we came in." Of course, Miche sweeping by with his silks and youth, vaunting. And in her kingdom, only women ruled with men. We were dangerous trespassers.

I wanted to go up to her and lift her away from the sordid restaurant where she had sunk like a stone. Take her through the city, lighting her cigarettes for her, helping her fragility gallantly across the rainy roads. Tell her I admired her, buy her something dainty. But such an impulse was most unwise.

When we left near midnight, she was still electrically alone at her table, ordering champagne now, a nice one. Keeping up the evening's life, not letting it go.

"Well, we got away before she stabbed you," said Miche, looking up at the red moon. "What did you see in the cow?"

I didn't bother to say. Flowers in their winter mode, soggy and half dead, their colors lost and petals falling, smelling no longer of anything we like. As we throw them on the bonfire we forget they had such charm. They burn and flash in the fire, gaudy, and brave, and that's the end of them.

Judas Garbah

"Why in God's name did she call you that?"

"She hated me. I told you, she was always try-ing to lose me in the slums."

"Judas," said my companion, consideringly. His own name was Georges, a perfectly acceptable one. He could, if he wanted, link himself to whole calendars full of kings and saints. My name's fame, of course, came from the Iscariot family, all those years ago in Palestine. "Did you never think of changing it?"

"My father did. Once he'd extricated me from my mother's limp clutches."

"Oh? So tell me, what name did he give you?"

"Something ordinary and nondescript, a drab, paltry little name no one would remark or remember. What else but *Georges?*"

My companion then called me quite another sort of name. But presently got up and came to kiss me. A reasonably amiable lover, Georges. At least to begin with.

Soon after this, our lunch was finished. Despite the heat we rose and walked away from the terrace of the white-painted house, along the track of burnt earth that led up above the village.

A few miles off by train lay another country, and a surreal town constructed of stone vegetables, something magicked out of leg-end. We hadn't yet stirred ourselves to go there, too busy with ourselves and each other. But the village had begun to bore us. It was full, as all strange places are, of non-human aliens, acting out curious rituals and routines like automata. One is excluded, and anyway afraid to join in. One wishes one had gone there in disguise, able to speak in the proper local accent and dress and stink in the exact local way, so passing unobserved. But it's too late by then. One has been seen, heard, sniffed, catalogued. But then too, after all, everywhere is another planet until one has learned to know it, following which you finally understand you are *yourself* the alien, the unreal thing. Not merely uninitiated, but a monster.

Some dusty stunted olive trees cranked up the track beside us. Beyond lay emptied fields, brown vineyards already stripped of any harvest.

In a derelict poplar a cluster of black rags perched, and let out a raucous yell.

"Bloody crow," said Georges. He crouched quickly to the path, picked a shard and hurled it treeward. It seemed Georges was sullen now, not wanting this walk, but unable to decide on anything more inviting. The vegetable town, and I, the two previous attractions, must have dimmed together.

Up in the tree the crow, missed by the stone, hopped and throatily swore back at him.

Georges bent for another missile.

"Let it alone," I said, less from kindness than irritation. "It hasn't hurt you."

"I *hate* them, crows. They're bad luck." Off whirled the second stone. This one also missed. The crow however, lurched from the branches and flapped untidily off across the fields. It was old, or so it looked, its feathers dull and somehow misplaced, its chiding voice like a rusty rivet. "Go on, you devil! Get back to hell!" bellowed Georges, prancing about. He had gone mad, evidently. The red-black wine at lunch, the pale yellow spirit, the roast meat of a fresh-killed boar eaten last night, the leaky creaking house, myself, all these had driven him from his wits. My name, even, even that. How probable. Here he was, having fucked the betrayer of Christ. My God, he was doomed now all right.

At the top of the track about an hour later, we paused to regard the distant mountains, where Cathars had been hunted and tortured and burned in previous centuries. Their crime: the belief that the devil ruled the world, while God was a benign and powerless being, capable only of promising something nice after death.

Going on, appropriately perhaps, next minute a sort of wood evolved and closed in on us.

The trees were crookedly black and skeletal, strung with a bunting of dark desiccated leaves. Through their gaps the distance and its images appeared and retreated, like mosaics of vision in the henbane eater's temporary – or conclusive – blindness.

"What a spot," said Georges. "Like a witch-wood."

It was. Yet too it was the sort of terrain more normally found in northern Frankish literature. Here, it seemed a mistake. And besides, what was the type of wheedling witch who might emerge from it, to kidnap we two innocent children?

After a few more minutes of plodding on, Georges kicking at any plants on the woodland floor, the 'witch' appeared.

George let out a loud silly laugh. At this, the 'witch' turned all his power of attention on us. He was an old man. How old, I'm no longer certain. To me then he looked about a hundred. Very likely he was in his sixties. But in that climate, and in those days, both sexes were inclined to dry up and to desiccate, just like the distasteful leaves on the trees of the wood.

He was stooped over, very thin, all in faded black. Like the trees there, too. His hair was longish and grey. His eyes a filmy black. His nose seemed either hooked or oddly pointed. He glared at Georges, who backed away and turned to me in visible terror.

I said, in a poor facsimile of the local tongue and dialect, "Good day, señor."

At which the old bugger straightened himself, and drew from the corded belt at his waist a knife, sharp as a broken piece of glass.

Not very long ago, I was sitting on a bus in London. I do that now. Taxies are luxuries. It's Anna, sometimes Esther, who have money. Poor impoverished Judas gets by as he must, poor old dear.

But to get to the point. I found myself sitting behind another old man (I was the first) and in fact he was undoubtedly younger now than I am, in his early fifties, I'd think, maybe less.

The strangest thing instantly occurred to me. The back of his neck, the *shape* of his hair upon his head, his flat, well-made ears – these reminded me irresistibly of someone from my past, that is, my *far-off* past. A man too that I had never known well, yet somehow recalled in the most intense and – I supposed – accurate detail. For a brief while I wasn't sure whom he could be. But then gradually I remembered the witch-wood. Of course, it was none other than the 'witch' himself. Had I recorded him then, so intimately, from behind – this smooth strong neck, without what my sister Anna has sometimes referred to as the 'Westerner's Crank.' That is a neck with a dent along the back of it, which describes the passage of the spine into the skull. Among male Jews, according to Anna, this indentation is always absent. I must say I've seldom ever seen it, save in adolescent boys, and certainly the man on the bus did not have this *crank*. His neck was firm and rounded as a column, crisscrossed only two or three times by a few neat horizontal creases of gathering age.

His hair was dark, but greying. His ears, I decided, were very couth, not small but neatly aligned. Nor had the lobes elongated much.

From behind, he was curiously attractive, and he had besides an appealing odor of cleanness and health, only accentuated by some powdery hint of his age. Partly I wanted to bend forward and inhale him, the nape of his neck, his greying hair. I was – to be frank – for a second aroused, in the most absurd and romantic way.

And so I recalled the one he reminded me of.

In that second too, like an omen, the bastard turned and looked out of the bus window. Not a bad face, but not the face I had unconsciously primed myself to expect. He wasn't after all the 'witch' from the wood all those years before, and just above the Spanish border.

Georges screamed.

The knife in the old man's hand glittered perilously, a nasty slender penis of steel.

He stooped, and began to dig out, from under one of the trees, a clump of stiff spikes, each hosting a single indigo berry-like flower. These were, I thought, the flower known locally as *blue grape*, though I might well have mistranslated the name.

Georges tugged on my arm. "We must run away—"

"Rubbish. He isn't interested in us."

"He's mad – a madman."

The old man straightened up, at least as much as his bowed posture allowed. He shot us a glance from the drained ink of his eyes.

His free hand, which was brown and bony as a bunch of twigs, made a gesture to us. Surprisingly it was not obscene. He had beckoned. We were to follow him, somewhere. Yet his invitation seemed to give him no pleasure. He turned his back then, and stamped away among the trees.

I had spent so much of my life following unsuitable people about, often unavoidably, I immediately went after him.

Georges rambled to the rear, remonstrating, until I told him to be quiet. I thought he would leave me, believed he had, realized he had not, and partially forgot him. Our personal idyll certainly seemed to be reaching its end. Until quite mature, I tended always to expect advances – many excitable and usually unwanted – and in the same proportion, inevitable rejections. Anna used to say my own envisaging *caused* them to happen. Now I expect nothing very much, and seldom does anything come.

The sunlight burned holes through the trees, which were drawing together. Then a burnt sienna shadow, hot as a cauldron, filled the woody tunnel. Down which the old man quickly limped, illogically pursued by me (and Georges).

At the tunnel's end, a stark hillside opened out into a hole of air. Below, the wild land rolled off towards the mountains. On the brink, like something washed up by a wave, stood an old-fashioned house of some size and dilapidation. Before it was a yard, with chickens picking about, or squawking and flapping up on the broken wall. A line of red jars stood there, and fallen all around were bits of tiles from the roof. The old man, not once looking back, crossed the yard, cursing the chickens in thickly ornamental vernacular. He thrust at a wooden door, already ajar, and lurched on into the silent cavern of this palatial hovel.

"*Don't,*" said Georges, running to catch me. "Don't be *stupid,* Judas."

I shook him off, navigated the chickens, and also walked straight into the house.

It was instantly underwater cool. So many of those places are like this inside their cave walls of stone. The space was wide, the floor also laid with tiles, also broken. A stair curved out of it, leading to the upper story. But a deeper shadow was in charge there, and the sickly honeyish smell of warmed rot drifted down.

Georges had now entered too, and fidgeted behind me.

"Those jars left outside are full of *piss,*" he informed me.

"It's probably stale wine," I said. "Unless he's a tanner."

"Oh don't be such a fool, Judas. Let's get out."

The old man in black had disappeared, and there was a choice as to where he might have gone. Undoubtedly not up the stair so fast. But three closed doors marked the stained, veined empty walls, and a single archway, that gave on a steeply angled passage. Some sense of light was there.

A svelte lizard ran over the tiles on little clicking feet.

Georges now shrieked. He wasn't afraid of lizards.

I turned round, and saw a short round woman, covered up in the familiar drained black. She must have come in from outside as we had, and seemed furious rather than startled by our presence. At noisy Georges in particular she cast a baleful look, and spat directly on the floor, presumably either to ill wish him, or to render him invisible. As neither spell seemed to take, she briskly clumped across to one of the three doors, went through and slammed it.

Georges wailed as I progressed into the angled passage. Its crooked arm led out into another high-walled area, this roofless and lit by the open sky. It was a courtyard, once carefully planted, now becoming ruinous. Small stretched dead trees and roping brown vines webbed the walls, in some of them little mummified fruits, unrecognizable and black. A dry fountain had a noseless cherub pouring nothing from a shell. The floor was beaten earth, sun baked, and scattered by what looked like the torn-off wings of insects scorched in fire. He, the old man, sat on a stone bench

against the wall. He too looked scorched, if not quite mummified.

He glanced at me again.

"*Inglés,*" he said.

I smiled. "No."

His eyes, tarnished mirrors. "*Judio,*" he accurately decided.

I added, "*Mitad árabe.*"

He showed his tarnished teeth, a grin, or a primeval signal of
rage, and lowered his gaze to the fistful of blue grape he was busy
thrusting into soil.

The sun was slanting over. A ray struck suddenly down on
the court, hitting the edge of the dead fountain. A strange noise
sounded. I stared transfixed.

Very slowly, the wrecked cherub was splitting into two. As the
two halves (perhaps like me, one half Jew, one half Arab) folded
back, a peculiar black creature slid out. It most resembled a salamander, a tiny dragon from some bestiary. Huge barbs or spines
ran along the ridge of its back. A pair of stiff black wings stiffly
rose up, the hinged jaw undid and out came a violent hissing that
made me jump. It wasn't I'd thought the thing was alive, I knew
it must only be some mechanism, but the noise was vicious and
I had no idea what to anticipate from it next. It showed me. Out
of the clockwork jaws rushed a glittering stream of dirty fluid
that splashed about the basin and over on to the earth below. The
emission ceased. The mouth clapped shut with a clank.

The old man was laughing, presumably at me. I took no notice
and went to inspect the salamander, now it was still. It seemed
made of black iron. Had the sun shaft activated it? Maybe. Or
else some trigger under the bench where the old man might tap
it with his foot.

Behind me, back in the house, I could hear a murmur of voices.
One seemed to belong to Georges, who had not come with me
into the court.

"He is in no true danger from Marija," said the old man, in the
local polyglot. I had begun to detect the more strident tones of a
woman. Marija, then. She was welcome to Georges.

The old man had potted up the blue grape, and now, alarmingly, he came across the court towards me. He walked like a crab, arrogantly limping almost sideways. His face was made of brown pleatings. He leant past me and rapped the dragon on its snout. At which it raised itself all the way up on to its hind limbs, like a dog begging. It had eyes of mica that flashed. "Made of me. I am," the old man said to me, with a terrible, implacable pride, "Cuerca. Patxi Cuerca. Come, I will show you, in my room."

In the house, Georges was hysterically protesting in French, "*Non, non, madame—*"

But had he been in the court with us probably he would have clung to me, trying to anchor me to the spot, and save me from who knew what worse-than-death fate the old man was plotting.

Unimpeded, I accompanied Patxi Cuerca. And what sort of name was that, if I had even understood him? *Cuerca* – didn't that mean *crow*? Or no, perhaps not. Yet he was like a crow, like the eldritch crow in the tree the two stones missed.

The Room led directly off the court. Through the round-topped door we entered a windowless blank, where something seemed lurking in a smell of spice and mould. He struck a match and lit a lantern which hung just inside. I had not even seen it. Then, he shut us in.

A child somewhere – where? who? – had told me about the chamber in the rock where the robbers hid their treasure and Ali Baba found it. The child had not been Anna, though she was quite capable of that. But my sisters and I had never met when we were children.

The lantern, a huge ungainly object, swung for a few moments, then settled itself.

It was a filthy room, into which a rainbow had fallen, splashing everywhere, even into the webs of spiders.

With the erosion of time, which can eat at the edges even of the most visual memory, Cuerca's Room is difficult to describe, at least in logical terms. It acted instead on the optic nerve, the viscera.

What did I see first? There was a stripe of pure green that hung and blazed as if with green fire, and rippled as if with green water.

And over there, another stripe, this one orange, that did similar things. And there was a crimson square that kept immobile and glowed like the core of a hearth. And curves of deep blue and purple that twitched and waited, and a slinking manipulative yellow, like a leopard.

He didn't advise me. He let me find my own way. I began to see in greater depth.

He, it could only have been he, had painted shapes on the walls in vivid opaque color. And over them and beside them and before them had been hung or slung, or nailed, or simply piled, objects that were of those same colors, either exactly, or in some corresponding color-echo. A bunch of green enamel grapes suspended from a green cord before the green stripe, an emerald glass pitcher, its neck smashed off and instead surmounted with a green-painted egg, stood below, jade grapes on a plate of green faint enough to seem transparent. Against the red oblong rags of a tattered vermilion banner from some war, a red cup holding an artificial rose like blood. Where the yellow uncoiled, a piece of ochre ivory, shaped like the fretboard from some giant's guitar, nestled in a cascade of broken yellow glass. Against the blue a woman's blue shoe, its little heel caught in a sapphire comb. A cluster of dried oranges choked by necklaces of chipped amber melted into the orange circle...

The old man, Cuerca, went by me, and unceremoniously and unerringly shoved the purplish grape-flowers between the violet colored jug without a handle and the chunk of raw amethyst beside the hoop of purple paint.

The expensive and the worthless clustered in each group as one. No hierarchies among these items, lost or abandoned, stolen or thrown out on rubbish heaps, all eventually pilfered by him, by Patxi Cuerca, brought here and each made part of its correct entity.

To outline all this is only to invite incomprehension and scorn. How could such an eccentric, *childish* medley convey anything? It did. No doubt the dark, flooded selectively by the big cracked lantern, caused some of the effect. But that hot day maybe my eyes had been thirsty. And now they drank.

The lamp flickered, some insect or cobweb dropping in there. I saw the yellow shape, crusted with its glisten, swing quietly sidelong to seize the blue shape – a woman, dancing – in its mouth. How gracefully she fell. But the red shape, stretching from oblong to square, and back to oblong, sprouted a thousand red roses, twining and knotting with their ruby thorns. The purple shape was a galleon's sail, marked with an indecipherable device. The orange shape was the ship's bodywork. They flowed together and sailed over the green shape of sea, which spangled and rioted with darting jade fish, spraying up the emerald foam—

But I thought of the spice and mold I could still smell, of drugs grown and harvested from the petrified courtyard, which formerly had been, had it, a Garden of Earthly Delights?

I blinked, once, twice. The shapes were static. Almost. Priceless and worthless. Unalive and living. They only shimmered a little, as the lamp had. Flicked a blue sequined eyelid or a sinuous tail. One last minuscule wave broke over the amber figurehead, who pursed her lips, before her face lapsed back to necklaces. The purple sail shivered as it flattened out against the wall. A single petal fell through the roses. Became again a broken red bead.

Quite suddenly then the old man, the magician, turned round, and the finale of his magic show was accomplished.

I saw him dazzling clear, meshed between the streams and orifices of colors. Like the salamander which had emerged from the chipped cherub, the real man now stepped free of his shell. Cuerca was young. He was straight, tall, lean, his shoulders back, his body planted as fluidly as an athlete's on his strong long legs. He wore his now inky clothes only in affectation, to match the ink-black feathers of his thick smooth hair, the jet stones of his eyes. His unlined face was handsome, nose aquiline, mouth long, slender and aloof. In his beautiful hands, articulately strong enough to rip out any beating heart, he held a burnished flame of knife. But you could not be afraid at this. You wanted all, and therefore anything and everything he might do. And he said to me, in perfect, only-slightly accented French (while the light glinted on his white teeth), "Go along now. Get out. You've seen. Go and rescue your friend from Marija. *Remember.* I am Patxi Cuerca. Never *forget* you have seen me, and this room."

And then, weightless and careless, as if casting a paper, he tossed the knife over my head. It thunked into some soft place in the wall behind me.

Disarranged by its motion, the lamplight jumped again, the rainbow leapt, and all its pieces, with the shadow, came down on him, and covered him up. He was old once more, dirty and crippled, and crazy. So I turned and went out, and in the courtyard the dragon too had slid back into its stony carapace. The liquid it had spat was already dry.

Although I rescued him from Marija, Georges did not forgive me. She had been telling him he was her long lost son, it seemed, and threatening him with the rich (seventeen olive trees) betrothed he had deserted, telling him she would bring him wine and he must drink it.

Perhaps he *was* her son. After all, I had seen the Room, and I had seen Cuerca grow young again, and then old again. Metamorphosis riddled the place.

No doubt Cuerca's youth was only a trick of the light, as they say. Or drugs burning. Or the dazzling after-images of all the colors sprawled about in there.

Around thirteen years later – also long ago now – I saw a photograph of him as a young man, in a book to do with the art of that torrid southern region. For of course he had been an artist of repute, when young. Abstract paintings, sculptures and mechanical toys not for children, peculiar gardens even, were credited to his invention. He did, in the picture, look remarkably like what I'd glimpsed, or imagined, standing among his last creation, his Room. (The book did not mention, or did not know about, the Room.) But probably, even by the time I opened the book and saw him there, he was himself dead.

As Georges and I tramped back to our rented house in the ash of the afternoon, he swore at me and I at him. Any liking was gone, and any tenderness. Which wouldn't, naturally, prevent an orgy of famished coupling for another two days and three nights.

When we passed below the poplar tree, the crow had returned there. It sat far up, raising its disheveled head to the over-gilded sky and rasping out a succession of caws.

Georges at once transferred his vitriol, or some of it, to the crow. "If I had a gun I'd shoot it!" And then to me, "I'd shoot you too, you damned Semite bugger."

But I only saw Cuerca's knife as if skimmed over my head; *Remember me. Remember me.*

Georges, immune to his own repetitions, was scrabbling for another stone. I pushed him hard so he fell flat on the track. When he got up, he followed me in rebellious docility.

"Bloody crow," he muttered. "Crow-crow-crow. Why do you want to protect it? What use is it? It's old and diseased and worthless. It's nothing."

The crow lifted itself out of the quills of the poplar. It spread its wings and sprang into the sky.

"Look, Georges," I said. "Do you see? It can fly."

From a fragmentary MS by Judas Garbah,
collated and adapted by Anna Garber, his sister.

DISTURBED BY HER SONG

Esther Garber & Tanith Lee

So the thought of you, remaining
Deeply folded in my brain,
Will not leave me: all things leave me:
You remain.

Arthur Symons Memory

ONE

All the time, when she was young, Georgina fell in love with people. Even occasionally with men; although in that case not sexually. It was around that time also that she began to dream about the green house.

The house (in her dreams) was unalterably located on a sort of rise or slight hill, where it stood alone, while other houses and various buildings lay just below and closely adjacent. These changed from dream to dream. One or two busy roads encircled or ran by the house. Sometimes it was positioned at a T junction, with three, though never a crossroads. Tall trees and a small wild garden surrounded it on every side, but the walls were low, or even in bad repair. And anyway the trees were often winter stripped, and only draped, as if for modesty, with a little ivy. She, and therefore anyone else in the dreams, could see straight over and through to the house.

Architecturally, the house was complex. It had, she thought, a sort of partly Victorian-Edwardian style. There were three (now and then four) stories, and a series of attics. Towers and long verandah-balconies ornamented everything above the ground floor, and there was – usually – a type of verandah terrace along the front of it too. Windows were of various sizes; some, on the upper floors, very long, rounded or square at the tops. Sash windows, or else the kind one threw open in two long panes like wings. At the summit, apart from towers and chimneys, a balustrade ran round corner to corner. Presumably the roof, where flat, might be walked on. The color of the house was nothing to do with paint. It was like that of a young healthy vegetable or fruit, an immature plum, perhaps, or grape, or a tuber of some denomination. The surface was luminously smooth. It looked strokable. Eatable. And over the crowns of its windows and the indecipherable ornamentation along the upper balustrade, a pale magenta showed, intermittently flowing in a definite if irregular pattern. As if ripening.

Georgina was always curious about the house during the dreams, and always recognized it as well. She did not, even so, always go in. When she did she either had a key, or the door had been left ajar. It was always *her* house, too. There was never any doubt. But it might be a house her dream-self *had* lived in, and now went to visit, or merely noticed, in passing through the (changeable) area. Or a house she had just purchased and was planning soon to move into. Yet sometimes also she knew, in the dream, it was the dream house she had only ever owned or bought or visited or noted – in *other* dreams.

Inside it was quite bare, but in good condition. The walls were of a creamy fawn, without faults. The floors of wooden boards were firm and clean, if not a *feature*, and *never* polished. A wide and generous staircase though, of dark wooden banisters, wound upward through the house. It had broad unsteep treads that promoted easy steps: you could run up and down it with total safety.

There seemed to be three or four large rooms on the ground floor. Above many more, but the dark wood doors were shut. Light came from somewhere. She did not ever trouble in the dreams to wonder from where. The ceilings were high. But in all her uncountable calls she had never explored any of it, (aside from running up and down stairs) except for twice, and these explorations both of a single upper room.

Nor did she ever find anyone else in the house, save only once.

That hot summer (hotter still in memory?), Georgina was meeting someone just off Oxford Street for lunch. The meetee was a boring man, a director she had known about eighteen months before, when she had been part of the singing chorus for a small theatre production of *The Bacchae*. The production had been quite good, however – credit where it was due. When she finally reached the restaurant, almost the first thing she would say to him would be, "I just saw Sula Dale working at the perfume counter in Liberty." "Really? And who's that? Shu-la Dade, I mean." "*Sula*. Dale." He was forgetful too: "She was in *Bacchae*." "Really?" "Agave," Georgina helpfully supplied the name of the play's only female character, aside from the maenad chorus. The director slowly shook his head. "What a pity. A good actress." He sighed. "Resting, I suppose. Just like us."

In later years Georgina would give up resting, to work more in the backstage capacity. But in the era of the lunch she spent a lot of time being interviewed and overlooked for small singing parts. Often work gained meant a lot of traveling too. Her last job before the meeting had been in Scotland. The meeting in fact, she had hoped, might lead to a London job, but it did not. And maybe for that reason too, seeing Sula Dale took on a mantle of extra importance. Because after, it seemed better to have had a significant cause of coming into town, and wasting two hours with the boring director, who unluckily turned out to have a physical interest in Georgina and had to be fended off before the third bottle of wine arrived.

Sula was anyway, at least to Georgina, memorable.

She was young to be playing Agave – her stage son, Pentheus, at thirty-five only a year her junior. Yet she had done it well, acted well, and spoken the translated lines in a musical and velvet voice. The horrible last scenes she – as a minor critic had termed it – *ravished*.

Her hair was probably a natural blonde, light-streaked and silky, her skin clear white. She had the flexive movements of a beautiful snake, an idea her eyes accentuated. They were 'hazel,' where darts of green-gold electricity constantly passed through amontillado sherry.

Georgina had, of course, fancied Sula Dale, and admired her skills. But no more than that, really. Throughout the three-week production they had perhaps exchanged less than twenty words, none of them of any import.

Perfume counters tended to make Georgina's eyes smart. By then in her early thirties, she could detect a chemical undertow to almost every one of the best scents. The same had happened to her with commercially produced chocolate. A shame. In her teens she had often lingered in both areas, inhaling these forbidden fruits. That day though, even as she was marching resolutely by, she glimpsed a slim, strong arm, lightly summer-tanned, and a flick of hair – not blonde but deep henna red. And knew, even before she *knew*, and turned round. And there was Sula Dale, smiling sweetly at a customer and handing her her purchase and the change, just like scores of others in the store.

There was a gap in custom then, and the other assistant was busy.

"Can I help you?" Sula asked Georgina politely. The sweet, interested smile was an act. But then Sula was an actor.

"Hello—" said Georgina hesitantly – "you're Sula Dale, aren't you."

Sula did that thing some actors do, instinctively sometimes, frequently malice aforethought. She literally backed off a step and composed her features to blank coldness. "Am I?"

"I think so," said Georgina more firmly. "We were in *The Bacchae* at the Coachhouse...about two years back."

"Oh, were we?"

"Well," said Georgina, trying to minimize the unintended temerity of a chorus member equating her status with that of the female lead, "I was one of the singers. You played Agave, of course."

Sula loosened a little. She looked now vague rather than guarded. "Oh. Yeah. *That* one. With Jack – ?"

"Dollington."

"That's it. I remember now. God. That place! A dump. And that persistent sneezer on the last night."

Georgina laughed. "Yes. I'm Ginny Kendry, by the way."

"Hi. So, how are you?"

"I'm fine, thanks. You?"

"As you see," said Sula Dale, frowning. "There was a movie deal, but it fell through. So, I'm having some work experience. "

"I'm sorry. I like your hair," said Georgina. She did not. She had liked Sula's stripy blondness.

"Did it for the film. They wanted to see it red. Then – zilch."

"I am sorry. That's foul." "Mmm," said Sula.

Exactly then a customer came over and wanted to ask about some new fragrance whose name Georgina caught as *Stupidest* – which seemed unlikely. But so many modern names then were weird or eccentric. Georgina pretended to study the scents standing along the counter front, little flagons of Benedictine gold, or opaque blue or crimson flasks. She sprayed a wisp of some tester on her wrist and then wanted to sneeze. She held it off by thinking of Sula's caustic comment on the last night audience. *This is madness,* Georgina thought. *Stop pretending and get out. She doesn't give a flying fuck. She didn't even want to know my name.* Like *Stupidest,* however, Georgina's name had undergone translation. (As the customer's preferred bottle emerged, Georgina saw it was actually called *Cupid's Test.* Which was also pretty weird.) 'Georgina' had been abbreviated endlessly, both by her succession of dire schools and the rather better musical Academy, and finally by various working acquaintances in the theatre and other venues (once even Glyndebourne) where she had, always in a slight degree, been employed. She was repackaged as Georgie, George, Gina, or even, twice, Gee-Gee.

And all that had subtly yet consistently annoyed her, until at last she always added to an intro, "*Ginny,* if you like." *Ginny* was tolerable. Even quite fun, here and there. "Ginny as in gin? Would you like a Ginny and tonic then, baby?"

The customer had paid with a card, signed and exited left with the awful thin-pink and squirted-cream box of *Cupid's Test* – what *was* it? Some kind of *exam* for gods?

Georgina or Ginny lifted her head as Sula warily glanced at her. "Sorry," lied Georgina, who was not, but perhaps should have been, "I'm trying to find something for a friend."

Sula regarded her with indifference. As a customer, clearly, Georgina did not count. Which must mean Sula did not believe Georgina's pretense at all.

Nevertheless, "What sort of stuff does she like?" asked Sula.

"Sort of – heavy, musky—" *Shut up,* thought Georgina to herself. But oh God, too late. Here came Sula Dale with a red flask, a yellow bulb like a scoop of poisoned treacle, and a tall thin menacing *shape* with a bow around its neck.

One by one Georgina would have to sniff them, even spray them. Her empathic eyes began to water. Presence of mind arrived quickly. "Oh yes!" she cried in false triumph. "I recognize that one. What is it? Oh. *Speechless.* Yes, she *likes* that."

Now I'll have to buy this rubbish.

She bought it.

As Sula handed it to her, with the very small amount of change from the ten pound note, Georgina wanted to say, *Let's meet for a drink later, shall we?* She did not utter a word, naturally. Her fantasies, until then, were all interior, and she was well practiced in their action, and their inapplicable rules.

She subsequently gave the scent to a charity shop. She hoped it would make someone happy, but by then it would be about a year out of date. Perhaps it would not.

Georgina knew that Sula Dale was gay. At the very least bisexual.

The actor who played Dionysos in the Coachhouse production had been incredibly handsome, and very taken with Sula. Members of the chorus standing at the bar after the show – Georgina being one of them – had plainly heard Sula tell him, "Sorry, darling. I'm like you. I prefer the girls." Sula had also flirted a little with the wardrobe woman, and one night a stocky but elegant brunette whirled Sula off to a late meal somewhere. Georgina was told they had been seen "snogging in the carpark."

So, it was not anything to do with *that.*

Sula simply had not noticed Georgina. And still did not notice.

All her life, then just over three decades, Georgina had found those who *did* notice her noticed quickly. And those who did not...did not. At the time of *The Bacchae* she had paid scant personal attention herself. And yet, seeing Sula again, bereft like that, enslaved behind the counter, Georgina changed as a ship's sail does before a suddenly altering wind.

Possibly it was connective sympathy. Georgina had been without 'real' work for several months. (Her meeting with Dollington demonstrated her desperation.) And then the image of talented, beautiful Sula, unchosen, wrenched at Georgina. What was wrong with everyone? Beleaguered against a foolish world—

The night after meeting Sula in Liberty, Georgina dreamed of the house. In this dream, just as in London, it was a very hot summer. There were masses of jade-green leaves on the trees of the stunted little garden. They made the green of the house into almost a plastic blue, while the ripening color high above became a sort of purple.

This time the main door stood ajar. Georgina went in, and swung it nearly closed behind her.

Her immediate feelings on doing this did not remain with Georgina, whatever they had been. She only later recollected, and retained, a vivid sense of energy, and of racing up the stairway to the second floor. And there, for once, an internal door had been flung wide open.

Georgina went forward, and looked into the room so revealed.

It was, you might say, furnished.

But what furnished it was this: a winding street led in and quietly downward in a steep slope. Buildings had begun to amass about the street approximately (as Georgina later calculated) some half mile along and down. What surrounded the upper part of the road where it commenced at the doorway, and the lower region midway along, she would not on waking remember. Nothing, she thought. Maybe just a type of localized mist, that in the dream seemed perfectly adequate.

The additionally odd element, which then she never questioned either, as usually one does not, unconscious, was that though the summer night she fell asleep in had been stifling, even eighty-five degrees in the tiny flat – which felt like ninety-five – in the dream, the vista through the door was wintry. She *might* have questioned that, surely. For the dreamscape too outside the house was full summer. But up here, in here, down *there*, snow lapped and capped the shops and tower blocks, and even the sheer blue sky was transparently icy, like an aquamarine left for hours in a freezer.

Georgina stepped out on to the road. Afterwards she had a skewed notion it had been cobbled, despite the drab comparative modernity of the '60's-'70's architecture below.

She did not go very far. It was not treacherous or icy underfoot, little snow there, only the faintest dusting (icing- sugar) between the cobblestones, or whatever. It was simply that – in sleep she knew it – to go farther was to become detached from even the dream-reality (the house); conceivably to be lost.

Which was quite crazy. For there was no menace in the view. If anything it was...boring. Like Jack Dollington, like Georgina to Sula Dale.

Georgina woke soon after this with an awareness of return, but no imperative memory of having escaped.

There was nothing to escape.

It was not a nightmare.

A week later Georgina had an audition for a new 'experimental' play due to be put on at the Figurehead in Richmond. If she got the job she would be the only singer. The music was atonal and – to Georgina – unpleasant. But it was within her soprano range. She had a good voice, which now and then could sound wonderful. Not among the greats, she was definitely gifted, certainly enough, she thought, for this solo role. She never thought she would get it though. But she did. They told her five minutes after she sang.

In a glow she rode the rattling train back into central London, and decided, with some proper pay impending, to give herself lunch at the restaurant where she had been driven mad by boozy, woozy not-wisely-choosy Jack Dollington.

In her own mind she did, presently, think she selected this treat because of the vicinity. And no doubt she walked along Oxford Street beforehand, glancing into shops after extra things she might now buy; new towels, some CDs of Handel, Rachmaninov, Joan Sutherland and Judy Collins, with this subconscious urge in the mental driver's seat. Naturally such an excursion was not bound to guarantee a result. But, just like the audition, it did.

Reflected in a shop window, there among the mannequins with their celluloid hair and hard patented skins, walked Sula Dale, a Dianic nymph in a grove of androids.

Georgina spun round (as they said).

"Oh – hi!" Georgina exclaimed. And then, fearing the quarry (was Sula by then *prey*?) might not hear, she added clearly, "Sula!"

At her name, as most humans do, particularly when they possess rather unusual names, Sula turned to see who uttered it.

What an odd expression. Sula looked *shy*. She lowered her green sherry eyes, lashes like dark mascaraed curtain fringe, as if *embarrassed*. Then raised them and looked at Georgina, full at her. And Georgina felt that virtually indescribable physical – or is it? – dissolvement of the pelvis, viscera and bones, which is presumably sexual, but which feels more as if that one part of the body has abruptly realigned itself with the non-physical Infinite Powers of gods and eternity and The All. And which, therefore, can be mentioned in any detail, generally, only in the most trite and ridiculous muddle of terms. All that thought, in a split second.

And how ingenious the lover – the *hunter*.

"I've just got some real work," blurted Georgina, feeling instantly a tactless bitch, for Sula worked in Liberty and not where she should, on a stage or before a camera.

Yet curiously, almost as if pre-programmed, Sula at once rejoined, "Oh good. So have I. A radio play. I've just been at the Beeb."

And then Sula's own relief instantly opened up the beautiful face into a smile. "What's yours?"

Georgina smiled tensely back. But lightly she added, "Singing at the Figurehead. A play with a crazy title...shall we celebrate? Can I buy you a drink – or lunch?"

Sula veiled her eyes. "Well—"

"There's a good place just along the road—"

"OK. Yes, why not. Thanks. Only I haven't got time for anything much."

So instead of the appealing restaurant they went to a sort of licensed sandwich bar, and sat on the type of back-punishing tall stools sadistic storks would have invented if they were so inclined. But there was Georgina in love (definitely now in love), and salad and ham in bread, and wine, and Sula beside her, and the sandwich bar became Paradise enough.

The talk was a bit sporadic to start with, but they improved it through discussing the merits of current Work. Sula's BBC play sounded interesting, and it was for the evening slot. She had the role of a woman still obsessed by the death of her husband in a car crash several years previously, who was then approached by a young man who appeared to be the husband's doppelgänger – an exact likeness and exactly the same age as her husband when he was killed – who next claimed he was the husband's son by another woman. Georgina meanwhile admitted *her* play was called *Evil Evening*. It was a five-hander that seemed to take place in an unnamed city, sinisterly and mysteriously deserted through reasons never explained. "The music," she added, "matches up just fine." At which Sula laughed. And Georgina felt a heady rush of joy at having, for a moment, apparently genuinely amused her.

All through the lunch, which lasted despite Sula's initial proviso, nearly a hundred and twenty-seven minutes, Georgina studied Sula, more or less without subterfuge. And every so often Sula would look directly into Georgina's eyes for a few seconds. During which it went without saying time stopped, and London grew motionless and silent and mysteriously, if not sinisterly, deserted.

Sula's hair had remained red, but it was more a strawberry shade by now, the henna washing out. If she wore any make-up aside from that on her eyelids Georgina was unsure. By about the end of the first hour, the worst and most devastating thing was happening to Georgina. She was beginning to see that Sula was merely ordinary. Even her grace, and certainly her pronounced beauty and extravagant eyes – were ordinary. She was mortal, finite. She was flesh and blood, had been born and would one day die. At this point a sizably smoldering passion can also die. Or else it will ignite. This one ignited. It noiselessly exploded. Georgina went up in invisible flames and a column of unseeable smoke, and lay spattered in bright embers against the eatery ceiling, staring down, lost. But she had been in love, even almost in this sort of love, before. And, like Sula, she had occupied a theatre stage. Georgina maintained her self-control.

In the hundred and twenty-third minute, when Sula said she thought she had better take off now, and insisted on going fifty-fifty on the bill, Georgina said, in a nice off-hand way, "Let me know how the play goes. Look," scribbling on the mentally prepared piece of paper, "that's my mobile number. Do let me know when the show goes out." "Oh sure," said Sula, not too non-committal. She might even mean it. Georgina added, "I'd offer you a free ticket to *Evil Evening* but really, I don't think it'll be worth your while. Probably not worth anyone's while, I'm afraid." "Oh," said Sula, surprising Georgina into almost stunning elation, "I might drop by. The Figurehead? Yeah. I once did a Hedda Gabler there. Not as Hedda. Mrs Elvy-whatever." "I wish I'd seen you. But well, if you do drop in – I'd love to know what you think of it all. It *won't* be Ibsen."

After Sula's departure, Georgina sat at the table drinking the last dregs of her coffee, unable for some while to trust her legs to stand her up. She was high, and cast down. She could see nothing but Sula Dale, yet everything else gleamed in a nearly radioactive light.

Fool, she thought, dancing over Waterloo Bridge, while the sun-starred silver foil Thames crackled and blazed below, somehow not burning up the river traffic. *Fool.* And it would have been quicker, would it not, to have gone via Charing Cross? But no. Let me stay in London. London where love is, just a fraction longer.

And Georgina wondered too if Sula had ever picked out Georgina's individual voice, there among the maenad chorus of *The Bacchae*, ever heard Georgina singing. And if she did come to Richmond, she *would* hear Georgina sing – solo – of course. *My voice is the best of me,* she thought, as sober with exhaustion she let herself into the miniature flat at Lee. *I want her to hear it.* Georgina stood still for a little space, watching the sunlight of late afternoon careen her small front room towards the west. Georgina remembered lovers who had liked, loved her singing. Two lovers who had often asked her to sing to them. And one who had dreamily said, "Angels will sing like that."

Then: "Oh, I'm glad you're *not* an angel though, Ginny"

I want to sing to her. I want to put my hands on her.

I want her under me and on top of me and her hair blonde again and in my mouth. I want her to smother me. I want—

But the phone rang, the mobile, and Georgina in her haste to answer it, because it would be Sula, dropped it, and so before she *could* answer it heard the voice speak and leave its message.

It was inevitably not Sula, but the director's assistant from *Evil Evening*, giving her a first rehearsal date.

To say Georgina Kendry never saw Sula Dale again would be to lie. Through the twenty-four odd years that followed their lunch, she probably saw Sula roughly about forty-nine times. She saw her six times in live theatre. And at the cinema in various movies, also watching these when repeated on her small TV. Later, when there was more regular income, the TV too enlarged and grew technical, and videos and later DVDs of some of the films (a few of which were very good, and one outstanding) came to inhabit Georgina's private store. Once Georgina was startled to find she had simply switched on the set late at night to behold Sula acting in a TV film from well over a decade before. How young she had looked when young. Sula also, during the nineties, had an important if short-haired role in two series of a detective drama, fourteen episodes in all. For a while Wednesday nights had always discovered Georgina home alone, and in her viewing seat by ten or ten thirty.

As the years progressed, the young Sula witnessed in the show from 1976, and the more mature Sula observed in the last episodes of the series in the '90s, aged attractively. She stayed slim and lithe, and her hair, though varying in length and style, remained a natural blonde that, by then, most likely was no longer natural at all.

But after this Sula vanished from the screens both televisual and cinematic; also apparently from the theatres of London. She disappeared entirely, and only in the early twenty-first century did a Sula Dale website manifest on the web, and so on Georgina's latest computer. The site was not particularly informative, in no sort a blog, or self-promotion beyond the most basic – a few stills and publicity photographs, a sparse list of appearances. She seemed to have moved to France. A pair of obscure French movies had her in supporting roles. Only one of these films did Georgina, after much searching, manage to buy secondhand. The quality was poor. It gave her a headache to watch; nevertheless she did watch it about five times, until the images utterly disintegrated. Sula must have been fifty by then. Despite the poor picture, you could see she was still beautiful, and still retained a serpentine body. But her face had become deeply lined beside the mouth and about the eyes. The marks of age on her, to Georgina (absurdly) seemed saddening and unfair. The similar marks on Georgina's own face did not bother her. Indeed, in her own case, she thought she looked rather better, older. But following the first viewing of the French film, she had to watch all the recorded TV and movies again, especially the art-house one, and look at Sula in her prime. Georgina never tried to analyze why. Perhaps there was actually no truly deep hidden motive. Just the fact that the lines cut into Sula's lucent skin made Georgina unhappy, *troubled* her.

However, at variance with all these second-hand, third-hand sightings, Georgina and Sula *had* spoken once, for almost an hour, on the telephone, about two years after the sandwich lunch in Paradise.

Throughout two subsequent decades, Georgina led her own life, and it was quite lucky, in its own muted fashion.

She kept her voice in trim with regular practice, and professional lessons wherever she could afford them, and it not only lasted, it strengthened, and extended somewhat in the lower register, as she moved into her fifties. She was still getting the odd gig even then, but as she aged almost always off stage, or in low budget films or TV background vocals.

Her mainstay employment had instead become, from about the age of thirty-eight, backstage work. She did not disenjoy it, and liked both the production responsibilities and remaining in the theatre world. She even wrote a few plays and TV scripts, originally in collaboration – to 'help out' – then independently. By her mid forties she had established a minor name for herself. She was solvent and had moved into a decent flat at the Oval.

Of course, there had been lovers, too. Not that many. Nor any of them incredibly significant for very long, but fun, or sexually or emotionally inspiring. In one instance all three.

Georgina had lived with Liz for seventeen months before a mounting acrimony, which seemed to grow *worse* the more the fun and sexual and emotional rapport increased (like a strangling ivy attaching itself to the challenge of a well-built wall) axed them apart.

Liz had been a jealous woman. She seemed to nurture this insecurity in herself. From the very beginning she was jealous of Georgina's interest in Sula Dale, evidenced only at that time by the stock of recordings. "Why have you got all these DVDs of her rubbish? God, she's pretty stale now, isn't she?" "Oh, I knew her briefly." "In the Biblical sense, I take it." "No." "You'd have liked too though, I bet. Go on, tell me. You fancied her rotten." "Yes," said Georgina in truthful annoyance. Near the end of the seventeen-month partnership, she came back from a stint in Wales to find Liz had cleaned and repainted the flat (then still in Lee) and thrown out all the Sula material. Or rather, was pretending she had: "To see what you'd do. And you've done it. Christ, no need to have a conniption fit. I've just packed them in a box and put them in the meter cupboard. They got on my *nerves*. *I* should be enough for you! *I* should!" roared Liz, having her own conniption fit. Georgina told her that the paint was too stark a white on the walls, she did not like it, and went to fetch the box. A handful of weeks after, Liz slung a glass sauce bottle at Georgina. Georgina ducked and the bottle livened up the deadly white decor no end. By three a.m. that morning they had permanently parted.

From then on Georgina was never tempted to live with anyone again. She thought she had not really been tempted to with Liz, only seduced and suborned into giving in. She had lived alone from her late teens, when she took a single room near the Academy during her training. She *liked* living alone. It was just the now and then company and the sex she wanted, loving sex if that was available, but honest friendly sex would more than do. Because since Sula Dale, even where Georgina still fell in love, it was never like the love that had grown up round Sula, and Georgina's loss of Sula. *That* love was like pearl round a piece of grit, or like rust around a blade left out constantly in the rain of unshed tears. What a flimsy context though, to have so overdressed itself. A few hours spent together in the most everyday fashion, one phone call, a host of fantasies. Why? Had the paucity of the liaison demanded this accretion – love, too, abhorring a vacuum...

And Sula *stayed* with Georgina. Really, Georgina did *live* with Sula. Slept with her too, wild dreams where Sula would suddenly burst through a wall and angrily shout that she would *always* be with Georgina. But awake, obviously, this was never so.

When Georgina sang, she sang for Sula, and to Sula, Every love song and lament, for her. Every book with a fair-haired heroine that Georgina read, was about Sula. Every piece of music listened to – Rachmaninov's Third Piano Concerto, the moon aria from *Russalka* – they were all about Sula Dale, and infallibly conjured her. She drifted from the mind's darkness and folded Georgina in her arms. She was like a haunting. She was like a second shadow.

Other (real) lovers felt her presence, even the least jealous. Even the ones Georgina carefully hid every DVD from, every inner memory. They knew. They scented Sula, they glimpsed her ghost. One of them had said sorrowfully to Georgina, "I know you

loved someone once, very much. I realize she must have died."
Georgina shook her head. "It's all right," said the lover. "I won't
say anything again. I promise."

But the dreams persisted. For all those twenty-four odd years.
In aspect they were diverse. Sula would burst out of solid matter or through a slammed-back door, scintillant with rage. Or
meet Georgina, smiling, (or mocking) on a street crowded with
people or a deserted woodland track. Or at the top of a tower,
where once she placed her hand quietly on Georgina's left breast
and asked, without either eroticism or aggression, "Where is your
heart? Is it here?" "I suppose so," Georgina had answered. But
most frequently in these dreams there was no contact, not even
a glance. Sula would pass by – or she was due to do so and never
arrived. These dreams, whatever their scenario or coloring, were
always of loss. What else?

Georgina never once dreamed though that she spoke to Sula
Dale on the phone, as in reality she had done, two years after
their last physical meeting.

Marc Henser's death knocked the breath out of Georgina.

She had not, by then, seen him for over a decade. He had been
one of her tutors at the Academy. He lectured on musical theory,
but the subject was not dry or overly precise, with him. By telling stories he would illustrate the pivots of his argument. He was
genuinely witty, clever, and funny; sometimes restfully abstruse.
An *old* man, at that time – as she presently learned – only in his
fifties. But in Georgina's thirties, when Henser was seventy, he
died of a stroke. Quick and clean. Or so Georgina's erstwhile
friend described it, breaking the news.

Georgina went to the funeral down at Eastbourne. She came
back up and then down from London again on the last train,
drained and drunk from the prolonged Burying Breakfast at a
posh hotel.

She walked round the flat and sat in chairs, crying as she had
not cried in the church or the graveyard. Marc Henser was one
of the men she had been non-sexually in love with. She and oth-

ers had spent a lot of time with him outside the curriculum. He always let his students be about him, without exploitation on either side. He would go on telling them things in the pub, as dutifully they swigged their Cokes and orange juices, or nursed their single wine or lager, too much liquor being bad for the professional voice.

Crying in the dark, lights left off, all but a single lamp, Georgina recalled his stories. How for example he had conclusively solved the riddle of what came first, the chicken or the egg.

"The egg, of course." "How do you make that out, Marc?" "Well, Justine. We know that every species started as something quite unlike itself, crawling out of the sea aboard the land. Then gradually it evolved, in some cases over colossal amounts of time, until eventually becoming what we know today – a dog, a lion, a man...or a chicken. Which indicates that the original progenitor of chicken-kind was remarkably unlike any chicken that now bears the *name* of chicken. Following this premise to its natural denouement, one must assume that, every evolutionary while, one of the proto-chickens would become rather more like what is now accepted as a chicken, but that the very last of these individuals was still not quite what would pass as a chicken today.

"Nevertheless, like all its ancestors, it mated and produced some sort of egg. And when that egg, that ultimate, formative egg, broke open, out came the very *first* chicken of the true chicken genus. Ergo, chicken-creature-not-quite-chicken, then 1) egg, and 2) true chicken." They had laughed and applauded him, making more uproar than all the surrounding alcohol drinkers. William had added slyly, "Egg first, then. I think he's cracked it."

When the sun came up out of sight from the flat, Georgina made tea, but was uncomforted either by tannin or daylight.

She found, in this unlooked-for extremity of grief, she wanted Sula. Wanted her now not in any obsessively romantic or sensual way, but as the child wants its parent. And as the child cries then for that succor and rescue, now Georgina began to cry for Sula, as never had she cried over Sula's indifference and non-return.

For Sula, obviously, had never called Georgina. Not about the date of the radio play – Georgina found it by looking carefully through the Radio Times each week for months – not about visiting Georgina's own venue in Richmond. If Sula ever had 'dropped by,' she must have been quite unimpressed by both the show and the singer. But no. Georgina was certain Sula had never been in the audience of *Evil Evening*. It had been easy enough to scan the meager gathering out front every night, before the house lights went down. And anyhow, the ridiculous play only lasted for ten performances.

While aside from any of that, Sula had *never* been, had she, welcoming. Let alone flirtatious. Sula was not tempted. Not at all.

Later Georgina was also aware why Sula so gallantly paid her half of the lunch. She had not wanted to owe Georgina, had not wanted to leave Georgina with any perceived excuse for Sula to repay the meal.

The dusty answer of Sula's uninterest rankled and depressed, but somehow it never gained a purchase. Somehow Georgina, though accepting and obeying the unspoken law that Sula and she remained unconnected, that Sula had forgotten Georgina, found that Sula did not go away. Sula did *not*, in fact, leave *Georgina* alone. Sula was always there, just to one side, just in another room – oh yes, exactly what they said about the dead. And in the dreams, even those endlessly repeated dreams where Sula would never even glance at, or speak to Georgina, often never even *appear* on stage as it were, still Sula exerted her power. It was like a spell, an enchantment. And reason with herself as she had, Georgina could not get free of her.

At nine a.m. that morning, Georgina did something that surprised her own self. She picked up the London telephone directory and looked there for Sula Dale.

To Georgina's further astonishment, she found that Sula was in the book, the full name too – not X-directory as Georgina might have expected. Many aspiring actors did this, however, to make themselves easy of access for prospective work.

Georgina sat and stared at the phone number, and the address attached to it. Decoulter Gardens – she believed she recognized where it was; somebody she had once known had lived in an adjacent street – one of those small squares in the back-pockets of the Bayswater Road.

Georgina would never diagnose if she was grieving most for Marc Henser, or for the death of her own former personality – her first youth, when so much had (erroneously) seemed possible.

That cliché.

But about nine thirty she poured herself another glass of wine, and called Sula's number.

Singer-trained, Georgina had cleared her larynx of tears.

She anticipated the phone would signal and go unanswered. Then the signal cut off. She heard Sula's voice. "Ye-es?" She sounded half asleep. Relaxed, sexy.

Now was the moment to ask for an invented person, apologize for a wrong number, put down the receiver.

"Is that Sula?"

"Yes," said Sula. Still relaxed, but more cool.

And now the invented character with a borrowed name rose up after all and became Georgina herself. "Hi. This is Justine."

"*Who?*" Sula's voice was now disbelieving, startled. She must have – of course – seen through the falsehood.

"Justine," Georgina repeated reasonably.

"That's really odd," said Sula.

"Is it?" *Yes, naturally it is. I am lying. I am using the name of that raven-haired contralto from the Academy.*

"It's my sister's name," said Sula, *now* sounding both amused and intrigued. "I was just speaking to her in Ireland, about five minutes ago."

Georgina laughed. A bright spontaneous laughter of relief. Such coincidences, *previews*, life can spring. Only six months before she had dreamed of Sula in a seventeenth century costume of scarlet silk, and some weeks after seen her in just that costume in a new film. This movie, which itself concerned the making of an historical movie, had been shot in Paris.

Sula was laughing as well.

"I'm sorry," said Georgina, "it's very early to call."

"Oh, that's OK. Sis got me up at eight. She would. Where are you speaking from?"

"Well, that's the thing. I'm in London at the moment. Makes a change after Paris, doesn't it. God, that was a good party. Where we met, I mean." (There were always movie-shoot parties. A safe gambit.)

"Yeah," said Sula. "They all just became a blur though, didn't they."

"I was wondering if you'd be free for lunch?"

"Not till next week," said Sula, easy as poured syrup. "I have to go over to Dublin. Maybe after the sixteenth?"

"Oh yes," said Georgina. "That's fine."

Oh yes. That's fine. That's – just fine.

"How about," said Sula, "l'Anchois? Do you know that? Near Seven Dials."

"Sure," said Georgina. Sure, the worst pub in England, the Tube, the local sewer, absolutely fine.

She could barely stop herself laughing again, but her stage control, which anyway was holding her firm through all of this surreal extended moment, as if really everything were perfectly normal, kept her on track.

And Sula then began to talk about the Paris film, and Georgina added pertinent comments. She managed to convey the impression she had had a tiny part in the movie, without saying anything expansive. Paris Georgina knew well enough to discuss.

And when the talk moved to theatre Georgina was on home ground.

They joked about getting lost in the backstage labyrinth at the National, and the bizarre freak sound the stage sometimes made at the Lyric. They spoke as if they were old friends, but too with a hint of something more enticing. There was a kind of display from Sula, the fanned erection of a peacock's tail – the note you might strike when you *like* the correspondent. *She likes my voice. The sound of me. She is hearing me for the very first As if I were singing to her. She has never heard me sing.*

(During all this, did any of Georgina's grief for Marc Henser remain? Perhaps. It was the somber key signature after all to these actions, even their result. She never felt guilty that she had – if she had – used her pain at his death to propel her forward. Marc would not have judged her. Though something did.)

They parted warmly, Georgina and Sula, after nearly an hour. The conversation had flowed. Something in them had become – engaged, even if only for that miniature space of time. As, through endless eons, a love affair conducted with maximum intensity for two thirds of a century, becomes also a miniature, when the winged chariot has gone by, mashing as it passes all such spaces, such *momentary* loves.

"I'd better go," said Georgina. "About one, then, at l'Anchois, on the nineteenth."

"I'll book," said Sula. "They get a lot of people in on Fridays. Oh, better let me have your number, just in case." Georgina rendered it. It was a different number by then anyway. "Well, take care."

"You too. And again – sorry to call so early."

"No," said Sula. She added, softly, almost like a child, (never to be forgotten, this tone, these words, fresh as when new twenty-four years later) "No, it was nice. See you soon."

Stars fall and cover everything with diamond dust. Dreams come true. Anything is possible. For a moment.

What on earth had been her plan? Sula would know the instant they met. Would Sula be angry – or flattered? Again amused?

Oh, Georgina would confess at once when she met Sula, to exclude all doubt. There in the restaurant, even before the first sips of wine. "Sorry. I just wanted to see you." It was a risk, but no, *not* a risk. Sula had been engaged. Things were different, different, now. And Georgina would be at her best, summer tanned, extensions in her hair, extra slim and fit from that last production—

Later, long after the event, Georgina had experienced a curious pang of conscience. Had Sula actually met someone in Paris she had liked, somehow not got to know her, let alone secure her, mistaken Georgina's fake persona of Justine for her? Yet in fact it could not have been that, not some mistake and keenness for a meeting with another. Because if it had been, Sula would not have called Georgina on the eighteenth.

Georgina, just back from having the extensions done, went immediately cold when she heard Sula's voice. The chill of fear she supposed. She had already visualized waiting at the restaurant while Sula failed to appear. Or better things, so much better.

"Justine? I'm sorry. I can't make lunch tomorrow."

"Oh. That's—"

"Yes." Brisk now, not warm. "Something's come up."

"Well, perhaps...another—"

"Sorry. Can't, not for ages. Don't know what I'll be doing for a month." Dismissive.

Yet it could be true. Events, offers, let downs – in their business – anything – nothing—

"That's a shame. But are you OK – ?"

"Yes. Fine. Look, I have to rush. Take care."

The lifeless receiver. Georgina put its dead body back on the rest.

Come, darkness...

I never saw a night so dark. Not a star, not a moon.

As if she too had died. Suddenly shot through the brain or heart, still standing there in the black sunshine, but everything finished. The curtain already coming down forever, upon the stupid and badly-written play.

TWO

The second occasion that she explored the upper room in the house-dream, occurred in those months that followed Sula's call. Georgina was writing one of her first plays, in a disorganized manner with a friend, and had abandoned all hope in it. (It was never ultimately finished.) At this time whenever doing anything else she always felt distress. She should be singing. *That* was her work.

She had become aware too that Sula had got into this play. Perhaps the friend was also aware. The lead female role, twisting in the furnace of Georgina's brain, into an attractive woman of about forty... (Eventually she would notice Sula appeared in most of her writing, as in most of the music she listened to. A role even specifically written for another actress would reshape itself, and Georgina would know it was still Sula, in the lightest disguise.)

That night, dissatisfied, she went to bed at midnight.

When she saw the green glowing house, she remembered instantly that she had been there before, and crossed the road to it. It was winter again in the garden. The ivy was thick on the trees. The door was shut. Did she have a key? Ah, she must have done, for she was already inside.

As she ran up the stair her footsteps echoed through the empty shell, but the banister had a rich polish on it.

She remembered too the room on the second floor; went straight to it. The door here was shut also, but she turned the doorknob and there, exactly as previously, lay the vista with the – cobbled? – road sloping down through a quite pleasant nothingness, and below, the buildings. They were glinting, not under snow, but in full late summer sun. It was probably about five o'clock.

Without hesitation Georgina went down the slope. She came among the buildings, an ordinary enough street. A little park ran on one side with tall (summer) green trees. Traffic went by. People, crowds of them, passing to and fro. It was a scene quite unexceptional, yet familiar, although later she knew she had never been in this particular place, awake in the outer world.

But then she turned down a side road and found herself in a pale grey square of large, tall terraced houses, most presumably now flats.

It was Decoulter Gardens. There would be the name up somewhere, on that railing, that wall over there. She thought she saw it. What did it say? De – C... Dc-ter...something. It was all right. It was the right address.

Until then the dream had been neutral. Now it became urgent and exciting. Georgina understood why she had come. She moved around the square, in the centre of which rose a single verdant tree. She stood beneath the tree and looked directly across at the building that held Sula's flat. The architecture, like that of the green house, had something Victorian to it. There was a balcony. How apt. Behind it, long French windows glittered in the sunlight. They were closed. But only made of glass.

People passed idly up and down through the square, too. When Georgina began to sing, some turned and several paused, to listen – this was all compatible. They maintained an orderly yet magical silence. No one seemed amazed, let alone disapproving.

Why should they disapprove? Georgina's voice was at its most beautiful, clear and silver-strong. It filled the air, needing neither a microphone nor any accompaniment.

She has never heard me sing. Now she hears. She hears the best of me, the truth of me, the soul of me. What I am or might be. What I could be if she could only see me as I am. But – she will. Now she will.

Georgina raised her face upward into the golden sun, the emerald shadow of the tree. She too was beautiful, here. Her beauty, like her beautiful voice, spread its wings wide open.

She felt in those moments, there in the square inside the room inside the house inside the dream, the unimaginable strength and validity of her own self and her life. She had not lost them, never could. Could never lose.

And then the glass doors parted and Sula was on the balcony, gazing down at Georgina, her face alight with admiring fascination and love, like a mirror of Georgina's own.

Georgina's song finished. (She would not, woken, recapture it ever. It had been a wonderful melody, and the words – they had been both simple and profound. But the lyric did not come back to her either. It was no song she had ever heard, or learned to sing, in the real world.)

All around the square the crowd, vast by now, was applauding her. And on the balcony Sula too, laughing and clapping, and then holding out her hand, calling, beckoning – *Come up to me, darling. Come to me—*

And Georgina, weightless, levitated towards her through the air itself, and then the dream, every fragment, floated from her.

She lay some while not moving, her face pressed into the pillow.

We know what we are, but know not what we may be.

Georgina never dreamed this dream again, not even when she dreamed of the house. But it would become an element of certain wakeful fantasies she had thereafter. In those, of course, Sula always ran down to let her in. There was always a happy, rational, explicable ending.

It was an attractive restaurant. A flight of stone stairs led up into a wide and well-lit dining room; tall marigold lamps by night and shining windows by day. Fifteen years ago the tablecloths at l'Anchois had been snow white, and the china bore the symbol of the restaurant's quirky name. By now the cloths were blue and the plates blue also, and plain. Always change.

She had started to come here now and then, in her late thirties, firstly with an American friend who seemed to have visited all the other places to eat, and asked her to recommend a special one.

When there she had never been so fey as to think Sula might all at once appear. Nor did she. But the atmosphere and food were infallibly choice.

Now, entering, Georgina glanced uneasily about. She had realized she did not really know who she was looking for. Or rather *what*. But as far as she could tell, Sula had not yet arrived. A few people were already at their tables, sipping wine or water, some peering through spectacles at the menus. Georgina had required glasses for reading since she was forty-seven, and would have to do this too. Would Sula?

How much *had* Sula changed, in fact – entirely, like the tablecloths?

Georgina had seen Sula last on film, fifty years old, in the French movie. She would be about sixty now. But the Sula Dale website had remained as uninformative as ever, with no more recent photograph than a publicity shot from the nineties.

She would not, Georgina was certain, ever have grown overweight. Sula had had that sort of body-type whose strong slimness is integral and usually lasts.

In any case, her fitness for *Winter Sun* must mean she was still, as they said, in good nick.

Georgina had written *Winter Sun* as a short story, the only short story she ever had written. Then someone at the BBC suggested it would make another play. And therefore a play it became. Finally its tangled path took it into TV, one in a new season of experimental drama. Georgina had been pleased enough, not least with the money. And then she had been shown the proposed cast list. "We thought she'd be perfect for Julia. Her agent seems to think she's free." "I thought she was in France," said Georgina, sitting in the wine bar that had suddenly been emptied of all oxygen. "Really? Oh, yes, but it's not like it's the moon, is it. I mean, the old girl won't have to go into quarantine or anything. At least one hopes not." *Old girl. The old girl.* Georgina supposed she too was approaching Old Girl status.

She made no objections to Sula Dale's playing Julia O'Connor in *Winter Sun* for *Drama at Ten*. And of course, anyway, Sula *had* played Julia for Georgina already, all the time Georgina wrote it. It was, the part, written *for* Sula. Just like all the others.

The time was, by now, a quarter past one.

Georgina had gained her table and sat before the mass of blue, which included a tall blue iris in an indigo vase, and a sky-blue glass of white wine. She had arrived a little early deliberately. She would prefer to be seated when Sula walked in, when she saw Sula first. Not be herself walking towards Sula, over this slippery sea of icy crystal, which was the restaurant's smoothly carpeted floor.

How long had it really been?

Only twenty-four – twenty-five years? A little less since the unique phone conversation.

How had it been possible – no, *permissible* – to remain in love, obsessively and committedly, for such a period of time, without a single contact? Not even to *see* the object of obsessive love save on a screen, in a photograph, in the enormous inner world of the alter-brain, the selective memory, the id, the dreamscape.

This is what happened, certainly, to the bereaved lover. Think of little squat fat Victoria Regina, mummified forever in mourning. But then, she had *had* her Albert. She had not had to *invent* every minute of their idyll. It had existed.

Yet perhaps an invented life also existed, came to exist in some aberrant way. As unreal recollections sometimes become a real past in the minds of the damaged and the mad.

But I am neither. And I know it is untrue.

But the love affair that has never lived, has also never died.

Apparently the audition was a great success. They had all been thrilled with Sula. Thrilled with themselves for thinking of her.

This had been relayed to Georgina. "Oh, Ginny, we're thrilled. We think you will be too."

There was going to be a group dinner, cast, production, writer, at some grandish carvery; Georgina cried off. Then the read-through, and again Georgina, who was definitely expected to be there, had avoided it. Food poisoning was her excuse. She could not face it. Would not.

Sula herself would not want Georgina to be there. But it was more than that. Obviously Georgina too had aged. She had got thinner, and only tinted her grey hair – but she was perfectly presentable. It was not *that* either. She was – *unloved.* She was *re-dundant.* Sula actually would not even recall her name. The whole thing would be disagreeable. *I am too old to deal with this. Surely I have grown up and do not have to.*

Georgina would see Sula in the accustomed way, on the screen when the play was recorded and complete. Was *this* the reason? Sula had become a phantom, a filmic ghost? It would not be feasible, or bearable, to encounter her now in the flesh. *Sula would be different.* Georgina would enter the crowded room and find another total stranger. Heart and loins would not melt, brain would not race and fire. Death would at last occur. The death of love. And after this – there would, once and for all, be *nothing.*

Near midnight the telephone rang, out in the hall of the flat at the Oval.

Georgina was sitting up in bed reading. She thought of ignoring the noise, letting the phone take the message. But now and then a friend might call from the US, or elsewhere, mislaying the time zones. She was wide awake.

She got up and as she did so, the answer-phone kicked in.

"Hello. Hope I have the right number. For Ginny Kendry? If not, my apologies."

Georgina stood, waiting. She did not recognize the woman's casual voice, though unmistakably it was an actor's.

"This is," the voice said, unfazed, "Sula Dale. Bar gave me your number, Ginny. I *love* your play. Julia's a wonderful role. Thought maybe we could meet up sometime this week? If you're free. My number is—"

After the voice was gone, Georgina still stood in the hall, still somehow waiting. For what on earth?

To know what she should do. But oh, she knew. Not now. She must not do it now. She would do it tomorrow. Or she would not. (Bar Smithwood should not have passed on the number without checking with Georgina, but Bar was like that.) *Does Sula even recollect she once met me? Why is she calling me? Eye on the main chance, maybe. I am a playwright with TV connections now. Does she remember? Do I care if she remembers or if she has an eye on the main chance – charm me, get another part to play—*

Exhausted, Georgina went to bed, and lay down in the dark. She approached warily, and from a vast distance, the former fantasy from her thirties, singing in the square to Sula's windows. It came to her with great vividness, stinging-fresh and shaking with hope and joy.

I am nearly fifty-six. I must not indulge this fantasy. Something I would never have done in the real world, even back then. Let alone, God forbid, now. But even to fantasize about it is, at my age, mentally – unseemly. See, in the dream I'm still quite young. And so would she be. And all that is gone.

I can still sing though. That recording last month for Peter. "Wow," he said, *"you still sound like thirty." Not quite. But I can still sing.*

Oh, what would Sula have done if Georgina had wooed her like that? Flamboyant, an actor's modus operandi? Lazy, careless, uninterested, exquisite Sula, with her hair like sunlit rain and her eyes like amber jade. Would the gesture, its crazy chivalry, its element of offering, Georgina's *voice*, have disturbed Sula's own complacent world, lured her out to look at another and see her, see Georgina as what she could be? *What I could have been – for her?*

She did not sleep, or only for minutes at a time, floating in and out of the fantasy she had tried to resist, and which however, now, would not pursue her back into the cloudy jungles of unconsciousness.

At nine-thirty the following morning, Georgina called the given number. But then put down the receiver. Then she called again and at once the slightly – not so very much – altered voice of Sula answered her. "Hi." It was only a touch darker, deeper. That was all. *Like mine, when I sing.*

Businesslike and cordial, Georgina said, "You called me last night. I'm afraid I was out."

"Oh – is that Ginny?"

"Yes. It's Ginny."

"So how about lunch? I want to ask you some things about your fantastic play, a couple of slants on Julia...what *you* think of my take on it all."

She sounds like a young woman. Full of life. Interest. Not bored at all.

"Yes. Why not. That would be," Ginny hesitates. "Nice."

"When are you free? Today? How about—"

"Not till tomorrow, I'm afraid. I can make it for one-thirty then."

"Sounds fine," said Sula. "Where?"

"Maybe l'Anchois," said Georgina. Or rather the person she had temporarily become, the one so busy today, as she was not, that one said it. So sensibly and quietly too.

"Do you still go there? God, I haven't been there in years, not even when I'm over."

"It's still a good place."

"Yes, of course. No, it'll be fun to see it again. All that comfortable old-fashioned white, and silver service – and the picture on the plates of the anchovy—"

"It's all blue now. The anchovy has gone."

"I expect all the plates got broken in some accident," frivolously said Sula.

Yes, Sula was acting also. Trying a little too hard, perhaps. Because Georgina might be so useful. That must be why. It could be nothing else.

"Well," said Georgina, "it was good to talk to you."

"You too – how are you, by the way?" said Sula, making Georgina jump. *What does it mean? Am I well enough to go on writing plays for you? Or you're just showing me a concerned friend from way back.*

"I'm very well. You too, I hope."

Yes, Sula was. A few more flutters then of mutual politeness and farewell, like a pair of pigeons fencing with their beaks inside a cage of boughs, striking the leaves with their wings.

In the silence after: Had the conversation happened?

But Georgina knew she was not insane, did not hallucinate. It had happened; a meeting was agreed.

As she was drinking very strong coffee, her mind ranged into the past and, curiously, detached itself obliquely from any memories, past meditations on or dreams and fantasies of Sula Dale.

She had thought of Marc Henser. Sitting there in the pub one night, when she was in her twenties, he, presumably, his late fifties, and the others, all of them alive, and burning bright. And he told them all the story about the nightingale.

When someone remarked it was like something from Hans Andersen, Marc had replied he believed it came from the eastern Mediterranean, Turkey conceivably, but that its roots most likely lay in China.

"Once upon a time," Marc said to them, with unashamed narrative effect, "there was a princess, outside whose high bedroom window a nightingale sang every night from a tree; a pomegranate, or perhaps a blossoming plum."

While the nightingale sang, the princess slept deeply and well, dreaming of wondrous and beautiful things. However there came a night when the nightingale, for reasons of its own, did not sing but flew far away. In the morning the princess summoned a gardener and commanded that the tree be cut down. He protested, saying the tree was young, healthy and fruitful. But the princess would have none of that. She told him that all that one previous night a nightingale had perched in the tree, and her sleep had been very much disturbed by its song.

One of the more innocent students had said, "But that night the nightingale *hadn't* sung. So how did it disturb her?"

Some of the others groaned. "That's the *point*, Keith. When it sang she didn't hear it. When it didn't sing she *did*, and it woke her up."

"So how was that, then?" said Keith. "Doesn't make sense."

"It's a riddle," said Marc, tucking slowly into his second half – he never drank more than two halves. "What do you think it means?"

"You don't know what you've got till it's gone?"

"In a way," said Marc. He gave them space to elaborate. But beyond a scatter of jokey suggestions ("She'd recorded it and left the tape on—" "She fancied the gardener and was lying so she could watch him sweat with the axe below her window—" "Too many Turkish Delights?"), no one claimed themselves able to solve the mystery.

"Analyze what the story tells you. When the nightingale sang the princess is reported to have had wondrous and beautiful dreams. When the nightingale flies away, and there is no song, the princess herself reports – not that she was *kept awake* – but that her sleep had been much disturbed by the nightingale's song." Marc once more waited. Then smiled. He had had a lovely smile, kind and wise and without duplicity. You had never had to think, *What is he trying to do?* He simply did it, and *all* of it was entirely benign. He was happy. He made *them* happy. A blissful contagion.

"When the nightingale sang, her song – although the princess never consciously registered a note of it – permeated her sleep and her dreams, and guided her slumbering mind into tranquil and enlightening avenues of adventure and self-knowledge. Like those people, for example, who can't sleep well or pleasantly without a tape of Mozart playing, or the sound of the sea.

"But when the nightingale was gone there was only utter silence.

"Think about those ancient cities and gardens. Not a sound. Today we can hear traffic, or emergency roadworks, or human hubbub, most if not all night. We get used to it. But in those sequestered palaces and times, the night might well have been an utter void. Like a cellar in the ear when the light bulb goes out."

He looked around at them. He said, "In that void then, the princess had no guidance for her dreams. They must have turned on her like a pack of wild dogs. It wasn't that she lay awake all night. She slept, and no doubt would have preferred to be awake, such were the nightmares and horrors that hunted her down and tore her mind in bits. And over it all, the *echo* of the nightingale's glorious song, the melody of rescue that never came, distorted and soulless, frightening – as some echoes can be – like the tinnitus-ringing in the ears you might experience after an explosion, or even, dare I say, a particularly loud concert. That then, was what she heard. That then which she wanted to render homeless by the axing of the unfortunate tree. But obviously, this would only be a psychological solution. Very likely it made no difference to her. Poor thing, she might never sleep sweetly again. And she wouldn't even know why not."

Was it fifteen minutes to two? Georgina's watch told her that it was. L'Anchois had filled up cozily. Just three other tables, seeming reserved and not yet occupied. Then a group of six arriving, couthly noisy and jolly. Over there now. The leaden feeling in Georgina's gut could be an awareness that Sula had stood her up after all. Or relief. Or hunger.

It had never been clear to Georgina why Sula had stood her up that *first* time years ago. Sula had not fathomed who 'Justine' really was, surely. There could well therefore have been a legitimate reason for Sula's withdrawal. Especially given the warm and willing mode of her original acquiescence. Or else she had just decided it was a date she did not need. Something more compelling, more worthwhile, had taken its place.

What to do now, then. Oh. Just pay for the drink and leave. To keep things civilized perhaps pretend to a message on her mobile, calling her unavoidably away.

She might as well finish her wine before she left.

Georgina turned and glanced from the window, down into the rainy summer street. Her pulse stopped. A taxi had drawn up below. A woman was getting out, was bending to the cab window. Slim, dressed in dark red, her shoulder-length, hair-dressed blonde hair falling forward – Sula. It was Sula. She was here, imminent.

Georgina drew back, not quite knowing what she did, and stared, as if to deceive Sula below – should she chance to look up at these windows – out along a narrow adjacent street.

Oddly (it seemed in those moments extremely odd), a very beautiful unknown woman was standing some way down this street, looking in at the window of a shop there, a flower shop, Georgina thought. The woman wore black, and her longish hair was the stony obdurate pure white that can only be natural, the winter frost of old age. But she was straight and elegant, and her profile, dimly, distantly noted, seemed clean and aquiline. How beautiful she was, how alluring, that woman. That woman who was not Sula Dale. How odd, odd to see someone like that, and to react like *this*, at such a moment, the other already on the stair—

But Georgina averted her gaze, and sat back in her chair, She too straightened up, and took a small gulp of wine. Any moment now, Sula would enter the room. Georgina fixed her eyes on the door, and held them steady, not even blinking. Like a soldier, blindfold refused, about to face the onslaught of a firing squad.

She maintained this position rigidly, until her eyes began to water. Then she did blink. *Fool.* Her watch showed her several more minutes had elapsed. But Sula had not appeared. Once more Georgina craned to the window. The street below was briefly empty. No taxi. No Sula. In the sidelong narrow street people went up and down. The other woman had vanished also.

A sigh escaped Georgina. Fate could always play such tricks. The woman from the taxi, evidently, had not been Sula at all. For God's sake, it was two o'clock. Georgina downed all her drink. She looked about to catch the waiter's eye. And then the restaurant door opened and into the restaurant walked the other woman, the old, beautiful woman she had seen outside.

The woman stood for an instant just within the doorway, posed with such poise and grace, in her slender black suit and her chestnut-colored boots. Her white hair was marvelously cut, it framed so descriptively her face. Of course – a waiter came at once to attend on her. They spoke. He had led her to one of the pair of still empty tables.

Caught in total mesmeric enthrallment, Georgina switched her stare hastily away. The woman too was gazing questingly about. But only for a second. She seemed unmoved by anything, removed. She sat down, and began to read the menu. White haired, older than Georgina, *she* did not require spectacles at all. Contacts, perhaps. Well...

Georgina must catch the waiter's attention.

She did not move. She sat staring, once more without subterfuge, at the woman who did not need glasses.

The woman's skin was lightly creased, and the lines by her mouth, above and below her eyes, cut deep. She had a beautiful mouth, softly colored. Her hands had pale oval nails. They were veined with age, but articulate, strong and delicate as a fox's paws. Ah. She shook back her hair. A girl's unstinted gesture. And abruptly her eyes flashed up again – truly they did flash, some effect of the bright wet day outside – and scanned the room. Georgina, who had just now fallen in love, (for the first time in over twenty-four years) saw inside the woman's eyes the light of a green sun through lenses of bronze. The woman was Sula Dale. And even out there on the street, misted with distance and time, and sight weaker than her own, even that way, and unrecognized – oh, yes, the dissolving pelvic bones and membranes, the familiar long-ago constant, surrender and desire, noiseless tumult, world's end. *I knew her. I fell in love with her again.*

But I would have known her in disguise. In a mask. In a decontamination body-suit. In a wheelchair, bald and speechless. Inside a coffin with the lid nailed shut. Even not knowing her, I *knew* her. In the distance, half seen. Through the rain.

Sula was turning her head again now. She was looking over at the door, with that touch of former remembered irritation.

But I'm here. You just looked at me. Or – your eyes met mine and then passed on.

What had happened? It was easy, though neither of them had thought of it, it seemed. Each had reserved a table, in her own name. So Georgina was led to the Kendry table. And Sula to the table kept for Dale.

But she does not know me. I knew her, even when I never knew her. But she does not know me. Never knew me. Never will.

Georgina rose. As she walked past Sula Dale's chair, Sula Dale glanced up at her, a fleeting glance, coolly courteous, impartial. And away. It was obvious: Georgina was not the one she was waiting for.

The waiter stayed perfectly amenable about Georgina's sudden departure. "I have to be in some meeting. Damn nuisance." Georgina paid for her single expensive drink, and tipped him. After all, she might, some day, want to come back.

Outside on the street she went by the flower shop, and crossed over into the main thoroughfare. Traffic growled. People passed up and down. Rain spangled like beads along the edge of everything.

So this was growing up. This was coming of age.

She would call Bar later, explain about the rushed trip to America – her sick friend. (Such helpful lies.) The TV team could manage without the writer. She would let them do what they wanted with *Winter Sun*. It no longer mattered.

Georgina walked unhesitatingly on, as her fantasies fell from her, quite painless now in the great tide of Nothing that already swam inward to replace them.

She didn't remember me. She didn't know me. She never heard me sing.

If Georgina ever had bravely stood below Sula's windows, in that square so contradictorily named Decoulter Gardens, and sung her heart and her soul out in a lover's serenade, *now* she was well aware that Sula Dale would not have run to her balcony or her door, alight with reminding and passion. Indeed, if Georgina had ever *dared* such an impertinence, she understood now quite bitterly well, Sula Dale would only have been exasperatedly, embarrassedly, impatiently and angrily disturbed by her song.

And down the glittering slope of the city then, grey and silent, stripped of dreams, the nightingale flew far away.

CPSIA information can be obtained
at www.ICGtesting.com
Printed in the USA
LVHW100851040622
720509LV00016B/282